PUFFIN BOOKS

THE WRONG PONG
PONG
TROLL'S TREASURE

Steven Butler is an actor, dancer and trained circus performer as well as a keen observer of trolls and their disgusting habits. He has starred in *Peter Pan*, *Joseph and the Amazing Technicolor Dreamcoat*, and as Henry in *Horrid Henry Live and Horrid!* His primary school headmaster was the fantastically funny author Jeremy Strong.

ABERDEENSHIRE
LIBRARIES

WITHDRAWN
FROM LIBRARY

D0306107

Books by Steven Butler

THE WRONG PONG
HOLIDAY HULLABALOO
TROLL'S TREASURE

THE WRONG PONG

TROLL'S TREASURE

STEVEN BUTLER

Illustrated by Chris Fisher

PUFFIN

PUFFIN BOOKS

Published by the Penguin Group
Penguin Books Ltd, 80 Strand, London WC2R 0RL, England
Penguin Group (USA) Inc., 375 Hudson Street, New York, New York 10014, USA
Penguin Group (Canada), 90 Eglinton Avenue East, Suite 700, Toronto, Ontario, Canada M4P 2Y3
(a division of Pearson Penguin Canada Inc.)
Penguin Ireland, 25 St Stephen's Green, Dublin 2, Ireland (a division of Penguin Books Ltd)
Penguin Group (Australia), 250 Camberwell Road, Camberwell, Victoria 3124, Australia
(a division of Pearson Australia Group Pty Ltd)
Penguin Books India Pvt Ltd, 11 Community Centre, Panchsheel Park, New Delhi – 110 017, India
Penguin Group (NZ), 67 Apollo Drive, Rosedale, Auckland, 0632, New Zealand
(a division of Pearson New Zealand Ltd)
Penguin Books (South Africa) (Pty) Ltd, 24 Sturdee Avenue, Rosebank, Johannesburg 2196, South Africa

Penguin Books Ltd, Registered Offices: 80 Strand, London WC2R 0RL, England

puffinbooks.com

First published 2012
001 – 10 9 8 7 6 5 4 3 2 1

JF

Text copyright © Steven Butler, 2012
Illustrations copyright © Chris Fisher, 2012
All rights reserved

The moral right of the author and illustrator has been asserted

Set in 13/20pt Baskerville MT Std
Printed in Great Britain by Clays Ltd, St Ives plc

Except in the United States of America, this book is sold subject to the condition that it shall not, by way
of trade or otherwise, be lent, re-sold, hired out, or otherwise circulated without the publisher's prior
consent in any form of binding or cover other than that in which it is published and without a similar
condition including this condition being imposed on the subsequent purchaser

British Library Cataloguing in Publication Data
A CIP catalogue record for this book is available from the British Library

ISBN: 978-0-141-34045-6

www.greenpenguin.co.uk

MIX
Paper from
responsible sources
FSC™ C018179
www.fsc.org

Penguin Books is committed to a sustainable
future for our business, our readers and our planet.
This book is made from Forest Stewardship
Council™ certified paper.

ALWAYS LEARNING   PEARSON

For Gavin Higgins and family . . . a very
West-Country inspiration for the trollish language

Contents

A Very Grizzly Grandma

Jaundice's eyes flashed like copper as she paced
back and forth across her cell in the darkness,
yelling furiously.

'HOW DARE THEY THROW ME BACK IN
JAIL! HOW DARE THEY LOCK UP LADY
JAUNDICE – THE TROLL THAT STOLE –
THE MOST ROTSOME SWASHBUNGLER
EVER TO SAIL THE UNDERSEA?'

Grunting, Jaundice snatched up her tin cup and
rattled it across the prison bars.

'LET ME OUT!' she bellowed. 'WAKE UP,
YOU GREAT FOOZLE FART!'

The prison guard, who had been fast asleep on
an old crate, jolted awake. The weeds in his beard
twitched with surprise.

'Oy!' he yelled at the furious old troll. 'Keep your
yellin' down or I'll –' Before he could even finish

1

what he was saying, the tin cup flew through the bars of Jaundice's cell and wedged in his open mouth. He toppled backwards in a shower of drool and broken teeth.

'LET ME OUT!'

A Weekend Down the Toilet

Neville Brisket raced into the bathroom and headed for the toilet.

'MUUUUMMM!' he yelled. Neville was so excited he thought he might burst. 'DAAADDD! HURRY UP, IT'S TIME FOR ME TO GO!'

Without waiting for a reply from his miserable parents, Neville lifted the seat and peered into the toilet bowl. Finally the day had arrived. He was going to spend an entire weekend with his troll-family in the town of Underneath.

Neville glanced at the note he'd found floating in the toilet water a few weeks before. It was an old scrap of handkerchief with the words 'NEV, IT'S BEEN ARMFULS OF AGES. COME AND STAY FOR A SKWINSY BIT . . .' scrawled across

3

it. Finally his mum and dad were going to let him visit.

'Stop shouting, Neville!' Marjorie snapped as she skulked into the bathroom. She had a face like someone sucking on a cactus. That, along with a mud face-pack and a head covered in pink hair-rollers, made her almost look like one of the Bulches herself. 'I don't know why on earth you want to go back down there with those . . . those . . . things!'

'They're called the Bulches,' Neville said over his shoulder as he practised wedging one foot down the toilet. 'And they're family, remember?'

'Don't mention their name in my presence,' Neville's dad Herbert scoffed as he waddled into the bathroom behind Marjorie. 'Horrible things, trolls . . . it's not natural.'

'And don't call them family, either,' said Marjorie through gritted teeth. 'It turns my stomach every time I'm reminded we've got trolls in the family.'

Herbert hung his head in shame and twiddled his thumbs. He still wasn't quite used to the idea that his mother had turned out to be a famous troll-criminal.

'Never mind,' said Neville with a smile. Anything to stop his mum wailing and gnashing like a slurch.

Marjorie eyed Neville suspiciously.

'Can I go now?' he asked.

'Fine.' Marjorie thrust a backpack into Neville's arms. 'There's a clean pair of pyjamas inside . . . and some wet wipes . . . and some bleach . . . and some tissues . . . and some *Stink-be-gone* spray . . . and . . . and –' Marjorie suddenly burst out crying.

5

'There, there, darling,' Herbert said, patting his wife on the shoulder like someone comforting the feelings of an atomic bomb.

'It'll be fine, Mum, honest. I'll be totally safe.'

'It's not that!' Marjorie snapped between blubs. 'I just can't bear the thought of . . .'

'Of what?' asked Neville.

'Of . . .'

'Come on, honeyblossom,' said Herbert.

'Of . . . of . . . OF ALL THAT DIRT!' Marjorie wailed.

That was it. Without even a backward glance at his sog-brained parents, Neville stepped into the toilet basin, one foot after the other, shouted 'Bye!' over his shoulder and pulled the flush.

WHOOOOOOOOOOOOOOOOOOOOOOOOSH!!!

Back in the Underneath

In an instant, Neville and his backpack full of cleaning products were sucked down and round the U-bend. Water gushed and everything went suddenly dark as he sped downhill in the water pipe.

The first time Neville had taken this journey, he was terrified out of his wits. But now . . . now he was filled with excitement. He couldn't help humming the theme tune of his favourite superhero show, *Captain Brilliant*, as he swooshed and splashed down and up and over and under.

The final twist came and went and Neville braced himself as he saw the open mouth of the pipe racing towards him between his feet.

'*OOOOOOOOOOOOOOOOOHHHHHFFFFFFFF!*'

Neville shot straight into the outstretched, grey-green arms of his dooda, Clod. The big troll stumbled backwards, then squeezed him in a big, troll-sized hug.

'Ooooh! 'Ello, my squibbly little lump!' Clod beamed down at Neville. 'Right on time, you brainy-bonker.'

'Dooda!' Neville shouted and flung his little arms as far round Clod's neck as they would go.

'I've been so exciterous,' Clod said. 'It seems like a month of mungles since I clapped peepers on you last.'

'I know,' said Neville. 'Mum and Dad were so mad when your invitation arrived in the toilet. Mum even locked herself in her room and wouldn't come out for a whole day.'

Clod chuckled. 'That Margarine is a funksome

one.' And, without further ado, the great hulk of a troll swung Neville on to his shoulders and started galumphing off downhill. 'We'd better get a move on. There's so much to do while you're trollidayin' with us. I've got all sorts of jubbly things planned.'

Neville held on tightly to Clod's shoulders as his dooda lumbered towards the town. There he was, after weeks of waiting, riding through the Underneath on his troll-father's back and feeling braver than ever. To think what a 'fraidy-cat Neville had been back when Clod had first snatched him down the toilet by mistake.

In no time at all, the pair had reached the stone archway with the words WELCOME UNDER carved across the top.

''Ere we are, Nev.' Clod reached up and ruffled Neville's hair.

Neville peered into the gloom and smiled. It felt good to be back in the Underneath. His heart brightened as Clod led the way through the narrow alleyways, past the rat-squisher's shop and Alopecia Grubber's restaurant.

By the light of all the milk-bottle lanterns, Neville could see the town was just as busy as always, with trolls rushing about in all directions.

'Home we go,' Clod sang to himself. 'I expect Mooma will be cookin' up something delunktious.'

They headed into the market square and passed beneath the ticker-dinger-thinger, the Underneath's gigantic clock tower – made out of junk and with numbers on its face up to seventy-three. Neville glanced up, his head filling with the memories of trapping his grandma Joan inside it like a rat in a cage. He still couldn't believe his own grandma had

ALOPECIA GRUBBER'S

turned out to be Lady Jaundice, The Troll That
Stole.

Neville peered high into the rafters of the
enormous clock, but to his relief, the old bat was no
longer there. He was just about to ask Clod what
they'd done with the gonker, when Neville caught
sight of Washing Machine Hill.

'Almost there, lump,' Clod said.

Instantly, Neville forgot about his grizzly old
grandma and his heart leapt into his throat. It had
been so long since he'd climbed the hill made of
broken, rusty washing machines to the jam-jar
house at the top.

'I'd forgotten how much I've missed this place,'
Neville said to the back of his dooda's barrel-sized
head.

'Well, you're here now, youngling,' Clod
chuckled and headed uphill. 'Welcome back!'

Surprises

'I could boogle my bunions!' Clod said, half giggling, half singing to himself. Neville wasn't sure, but he thought his dooda might even be skipping as they reached the jam-jar house.

Clod put Neville down among the washing-machine parts and hurried through the green curtain. 'This way, Nev!'

Neville watched Clod's grey-green shape through the jam-jar walls as he clomped across the kitchen to another grey-green shape. This one was larger than Clod and had a lot more hair.

Mooma, Neville said to himself and darted through the green curtain in his dooda's wake.

Neville felt dizzy with excitement. Suddenly seeing the Bulches' house again and smelling Malaria's cooking almost knocked him over with happiness. He looked around the kitchen.

There was the table made from stacks of newspapers and a splintered door, the broken plates on the shelves and Rabies the giant troll-mole gnawing on a bone in the corner. Pong, Neville's troll-brother, was licking a bowl on a barrel seat. He took one look at Neville and cooed loudly. Malaria Bulch was bending over the stove, wrestling what looked like a giant woodlouse into a saucepan.

'GET BACK IN THERE AND COOK!' she yelled at the ugly creature. Then she smacked it with the round end of a rusty ladle and slammed the lid shut. 'AND DON'T COME OUT TILL YOU'RE CRISPY!'

'Mooma!' Neville shouted, flinging his arms wide.

Malaria spun round, clasping both spade-sized hands to her chest.

'Oh, my grumpious little grumplet!' she cried. 'You made me jumpy. I wasn't expectin' you two back for yonkers.'

'Ole Nev don't waste no time,' said Clod proudly. 'He's all prompty.'

Neville ran and hugged his mooma round one of her hefty thighs.

'I've missed you, my brandyburp, but look at you,' Malaria said, picking him up and planting a wet kiss on the top of his head. 'You're scrawnier than a punker's poker. What is that Margarine feedin' you?'

'Last night she made us tofu burgers,' Neville said, pulling a face.

'*What?*'

If she wasn't grey-green already, Neville could have sworn his mooma just turned greener.

'That's just plain old rotsome,' Malaria said. 'I'd say it's time you had a Bulch Family din-dins and we'll talk about what funly things we've got planned. Eh, Clod?'

'Sounds goodly to me,' said Clod, plonking

himself at the table. 'Carryin' overlings is hungry work and that's no mistakin'.'

'Down you pop, lump,' Malaria said, pulling a barrel up to the table for Neville to sit on. 'Now you rest your bumly bits and I'll rustle up somethin' tinkly. I'll just fetch Rubella.'

Neville felt his stomach tighten into a knot. He knew his troll-sister, Rubella, would be around for his stay in the Underneath, but why did she still make him feel so nervous? He took a deep breath and imagined himself in green pants like Captain Brilliant. That always made him feel much braver.

'RUBELLA!' yelled Malaria, as she pounded on the ceiling with a broom handle. 'OY, BELLY!'

'What?' a voice shouted from the floor above. A shiver ran down Neville's spine at the sound of it.

'NEV'S HERE,' Malaria yelled again.

'So?' Rubella grunted through the floor.

'WE'RE 'AVIN' SOME DIN-DINS!'

CCCCRRRRRRAAAAAAAAAAAASSSSSSSSSSHHH-HHHH!

The whole house shook as Rubella burst through the ceiling in a shower of floorboards and bits of jam jar. The first time Neville had ever met the

enormous rhinoceros that was his troll-sister, she
had punched a hole in the ceiling to get a better
look at him. But now she came through the kitchen
roof entirely and landed perfectly on a barrel seat
at the table in between Pong and Neville, like a
hungry boulder.

'Belly,' Clod said, scraping a huge lump of
ceiling off the table. 'You could have used the stairs.'

'Too tired,' Rubella grunted. Then she turned
her huge, ugly head and leered at Neville. ''Ello,
whelp,' she said.

Neville smiled a nervous smile and tried not to
wet himself.

'Erm . . . hello, Rubella . . .' he mumbled, then

busied himself with picking bits of plaster out of his jumper.

'Dinner's 'ere,' Malaria said, clomping over from the stove with a tray filled with bubbling pots and pans. It was like she hadn't even noticed the whoppsy great chunker that had just plummeted through the ceiling and landed exactly in her place at the table. 'Eat up, Nev.'

Before he knew it, Neville was tucking into plates of very crispy woodlouse and hot, steaming mugs of left-sock stew. Even though he knew he should find it disgusting, like he had on his first visit to the Bulches, Neville loved every mouthful of Malaria's squibbly cooking.

'Well, Nev!' Clod said, rubbing his spade-sized hands together. 'We've got lots to do while you're here.'

'Absolunkly,' Malaria joined in. 'We can go for a stroll round the market, maybe.'

'And I thought we might go and watch some theatricals,' said Clod.

'The market and the theatre?' huffed Rubella, with a mouthful of rat patty. 'BORIN'! Tell the little snot what we're doing in the morrow.'

'Rubella!' Clod snapped. 'That's meant to be a surprise.'

'What is?' asked Neville.

'It's nuffin',' said Clod. 'Well . . . erm . . .'

'Why won't you tell me?' Neville said. Butterflies started fluttering around inside his belly. 'Is it something horrible?'

'Oh, go on, Clod,' Malaria said. 'Now you're scaring the poor lump. He looks all nervish.'

'Ha ha!' Clod beamed. 'All rightsy. Tomorrow, we're takin' you to visit the Clunk.'

'The *what?*' Neville said. He didn't like the sound of it.

'The Clunk!' said Clod, scooping another fistful of food into his mouth. 'We couldn't keep Lady Jaundice trapped inside the ticker-dinger-thinger, and what with us underlings being usually goodly, honourous types, there didn't have no prisons strong enough to hold her, she always escaped. So we built the Clunk. Everyone pitched in.'

Neville's heart started racing.

'You mean we're going to visit my grandmooma?'

'Indeedy!' Clod yelled happily.

'My evil gonker grandmooma that hates me?'

'S'right!' said Malaria. 'It's awful funly. We all go and have a good look and a fun-poke every now and again.'

'Where is the Clunk?' said Neville. He could feel little beads of sweat forming on his forehead.

'That's the other surprise,' said Clod, jumping up and waving his arms. 'It's on an island in the middle of the Undersea!'

'The . . . the Undersea?' Neville whispered. He hated water. He'd even failed his 'One width of the pool' swimming certificate.

'You're so adventurable,' Clod said. 'I bet you can't wait to get out across the big wetty ocean.'

Neville opened his mouth . . . closed it . . . opened it again and fainted.

Rubella pointed and laughed.

Bedtime Stories

Neville woke up lying on the pile of stinking laundry in Rubella's room.

'Oh, there you are, youngling,' came Clod's voice. 'I was worried you'd gone and popped your cogs.'

Neville scratched his head, adjusted his glasses and looked around the room. Clod came into view, sitting beside him. Rubella was in her hammock, reading her troll teen magazine.

'What happened?' asked Neville.

'You got so excited about crossin' the Undersea to visit your grandmooma Jaundice, you got a wee bit wobbly.'

Neville suddenly remembered what tomorrow's plans were and wished he hadn't asked.

'You'll love it,' Clod said. 'My dooda used to sail the big wetty when he was a bit fresher . . . and his dooda before that.'

Neville smiled a pathetic smile. Before today, he hadn't even known there was an underground ocean and now he had to sail across it. Neville groaned inside. Clod looked so excited, how could he say no?

'I think there's time for one of my dooda's old sea yarns before bed,' Clod said.

'Oh, lummy,' lied Neville.

'I love stringish things,' Rubella said greedily from her hammock.

'Not yarn-yarn,' said Clod. 'Fables and foobles . . . Ain't nothin' like a good bedtime story.'

'Oh,' said Rubella and returned to her magazine.

'Right then,' said Clod, scratching his head. 'Where to start? Oh, I know . . . My dooda once saw a fish so big it ate a whole town right off the coast, it did. All in one whoppsy great chomplet.'

Neville eyed his dooda and wished he would stop talking about it. He wasn't sure his nerves could take this.

Rubella could tell that Neville was getting nervous.

'What else did Grandooda see?' she asked, sticking her tongue out at Neville.

'Well, there's electric skrunts,' said Clod. 'They can sizzle you like a rat patty in no time flat.'

Electric skrunts? Fish big enough to eat a town? Neville curled his toes under and tried not to listen.

'There's the hundred-armed clonktopus . . . nasty, big grunchers, those.'

Neville whimpered. Rubella giggled.

'Glugulars and squiggers and pinchy little prawks that'll chew off your toes if you ain't careful. Then there was the time my dooda sailed across the big wetty in search of –'

'SHUT UP!' Rubella suddenly barked. Everybody jumped. She was enjoying the stories all the time they were scaring Neville, but she didn't want to hear her grandooda's life history. 'You're borin' me now.'

'All rightsy,' Clod said, clambering back to his feet. 'I expect you'll be wantin' to have a wee snizzle and snore, anywho, eh, Nev?'

Neville nodded. Anything to stop his dooda from telling more stories about terrible beasts in the sea they were going to cross. He buried himself deep into the laundry pile.

'Well, nighty-nighty, you two,' said Clod, heading

for the door. 'See you bright and bungly in the morrow.'

Rubella blew out the bedside lantern and slumped on to her back.

'Sweet dreams, Nev,' she snickered in the darkness. 'Sleep tight . . . Don't let the sea monsters bite.'

Old Barnacle's Boat Tours

After a hurried breakfast of pickled fish eyes and shrimp-scale tea, Clod led the group beyond Washing Machine Hill to a maze of alleyways on the far side of town. Neville noticed with growing fear that the way ahead was getting darker and more cramped the further they went, and everything seemed to be covered in mould.

'Hmmmm.' Clod sighed contentedly. 'Can you smell it, Nev?'

'Smell what?' said Neville from Clod's shoulders, but he could smell it. It was the unmistakable salty smell of the sea.

Neville braced himself and thought of Captain

Brilliant. He was pretty sure visiting the Clunk was going to be worse than the bog of the slurches, the dooky hole and all the other nasty parts of the Underneath that he'd visited, all rolled into one.

They rounded the corner by a huge stack of old, rusted motorcars and Neville almost toppled backwards off Clod's shoulders with shock. There, bigger and more menacing than Neville could have imagined, was . . . WAS . . . AN OCEAN . . . A GREAT, BIG, WET, ROLLING, UNDERGROUND OCEAN!

'*Ta dah!*' Clod yelled with pride, putting Neville down on the ground. 'Didn't I say you'd love it?'

Neville stood at the foot of a narrow jetty that zigzagged its way across the water like a rickety wooden vein. There were hundreds of them, but the jetty that Clod had brought them to was longer than all the others and there seemed to be some type of hut or small house at the end of it.

'That's where we're goin',' said
Clod. He was pointing at the little
building. 'You're the leader, Nev.
Steady as you go.'

Neville eyed the way ahead
nervously and prodded the first board
with his toe. The rotten wood groaned
beneath his foot and made a
splintering sound.

'Go on, lump,' said Clod. 'Nothin'
to worry about.'

Neville gulped. 'OK, Dooda,' he
said, trying to sound brave. He could
barely move. His legs weren't listening
to what he was telling them to do and
his knees wouldn't stop shaking.

'Off you go then,' Clod coaxed
again.

Neville broke out in a cold sweat.
It all looked so dangerous. On either
side of the jetty, the skeletons of old
troll fishing boats creaked with the
tide, and through the cracks Neville
could see the shallows below were

26

teeming with strange fish and spiny
crustaceans. They slapped the water
as they wriggled and clambered up
the dockside. Neville cringed. The
thought of landing among all those
slippery creepy-crawlies made his
skin shiver.

'HURRY UP!' Rubella shouted
from behind. 'MOVE IT, YOU
SQUIRMER!'

'Come on,' Neville said to
himself. 'Be brave. Remember
you've got troll blood.'

'What's keepin' you, Nev?' asked
Malaria.

What was he going to do? If he
chickened out, Rubella would make
fun of him forever. Before he had
time to change his mind, Neville
took a deep breath and skittered
along the jetty, praying to Captain
Brilliant that he wouldn't end up
going through it. He jumped quickly
from plank to plank and kept his

eyes locked firmly on the little shed at the end. *Keep going*, he thought. *Just keep going*.

Before he knew it, Neville had crossed almost the entire length of the walkway with his troll-family stumbling along behind. But the closer he got to the shed, the more he couldn't quite tell what he was looking at. The walls and squat roof seemed to be shifting and changing shape.

Neville stopped in his tracks and stared. It was like he was looking at a mirage.

'Dooda,' Neville said. 'What's that?'

'What's what?' asked Clod.

'THAT!'

'That?' Clod chuckled. 'That's the boatman's place. Can't cross the Undersea without a boat, lump. We'd all get sogsome.'

'But why's it moving?' Neville asked.

'Oh,' said Clod. He plodded over to a big dented bell dangling from a pole, grabbed the rope that was hanging beneath and twanged it as hard as he could.

DIIIIIIIIIINNNNNNNNNNGGGGGGGGGG!

'Now just you watch,' Clod said as the ear-splitting peal echoed across the waterfront. Instantly the walls of the boathouse started trembling more than ever. Neville gasped as he realized what he was looking at. The walls weren't moving at all, they were covered in thousands upon thousands of crabs and urchins and sea slugs. They scuttled down in all directions until, in no time at all, the building emerged.

'Ha ha!' Clod yelled, clapping. 'I love it when they do that.'

Carefully, Neville stepped a little closer, kicking aside the last remaining crabs that *click-clack*ed about on the jetty. The place looked like it had been abandoned years ago and was very close to collapsing into the sea.

'Are you sure this is right?' Neville said. 'It looks . . . empty.'

'Yep,' said Clod. 'Look.'
He pointed to a driftwood sign hanging above the red door with the words OLD BARNACLE'S BOAT TOURS  painted across it. Neville read it out loud, then knocked softly. His heart was thumping against his ribs. This place gave him the creeps.

'Nothing,' said Neville when no one answered.

'Try again, Nev,' Clod said. 'Give it some welly.'

Neville knocked again, a little harder this time.

'It doesn't look like anybody's home,' he said.

'Oh, nonkumbumps,' Malaria said. 'You've just got to do it right.' She reached past Neville and pounded on the door so hard the entire building creaked, then leaned to one side at an alarming angle.

'WHHHHAAAAAAATTTT?'

Suddenly an upstairs window flew open and a head on the end of a long wrinkly neck poked out like a demented cuckoo clock. Everybody jumped, including Rubella. She dropped Pong on to the boards with a soggy *thud*. Pong laughed wildly.

'WHO'S A-KNOCKIN'?' huffed the old troll. He lifted an enormous, rusty ear trumpet to his ear. 'EH?'

'Oh, there you are,' said Clod.

'WHAT?' Old Barnacle's name was no exaggeration. He was the oldest troll Neville had ever seen. Old Barnacle's face was like a pie crust that had been baked too long, and the seaweed beard that sprouted from his chin reached all the way down to the floor.

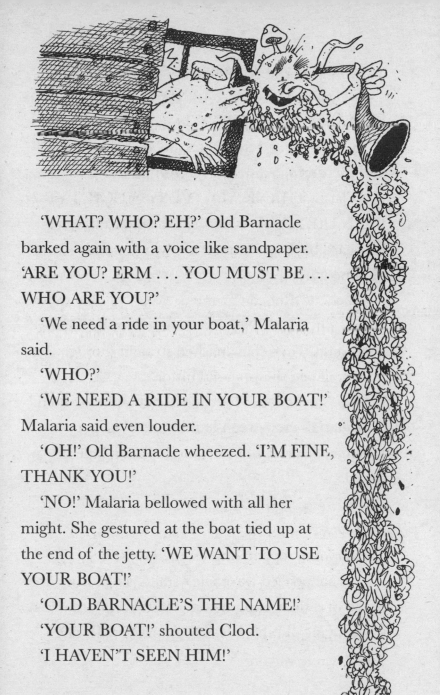

'WHAT? WHO? EH?' Old Barnacle
barked again with a voice like sandpaper.
'ARE YOU? ERM . . . YOU MUST BE . . .
WHO ARE YOU?'

'We need a ride in your boat,' Malaria
said.

'WHO?'

'WE NEED A RIDE IN YOUR BOAT!'
Malaria said even louder.

'OH!' Old Barnacle wheezed. 'I'M FINE,
THANK YOU!'

'NO!' Malaria bellowed with all her
might. She gestured at the boat tied up at
the end of the jetty. 'WE WANT TO USE
YOUR BOAT!'

'OLD BARNACLE'S THE NAME!'

'YOUR BOAT!' shouted Clod.

'I HAVEN'T SEEN HIM!'

31

'YOUR BOAT!!' shouted Neville.

'OH, NO, I CAN'T STAND THE STUFF . . .
IT MAKES ME BLURTY, IT DOES!'

Rubella planted her feet wide, balled her hands
into fists and screamed, 'BOOOOAAATTT!'

'WELL, THANK YOU VERY MUCH, I'VE
BEEN DIETING!' With that, the old troll reeled
his beard back up through the window and
slammed the shutter.

'*That's it!*' Rubella grunted. 'MOVE!' She shoved
Neville out of the way and stomped towards the
boathouse. Then she smashed straight through the
front wall and disappeared inside.

'Aha,' said Clod. He reached out and took hold
of Malaria's grey-green hand. 'She's like her
mooma.' Malaria blushed and looked a little bit
proud.

*THUD . . . THUD . . . THUD . . . THUD . . .
THUD . . .*

Everyone stopped and listened to Rubella
lumbering up Old Barnacle's stairs. Then came the
sound of a door banging open and Old Barnacle's
voice saying, 'I NEVER KNEW YOU LIVED
'ERE!'

'SHUT UP!' Rubella's voice barked.

THUD . . . THUD . . . THUD . . . THUD . . .
THUD . . .

Rubella clomped downstairs and back out through the troll-shaped hole she'd left on her way in. She had Old Barnacle slung over her shoulder, still clutching his ear trumpet. Clod stepped in close and cleared his throat.

"ELLO, OLD BARNACLE,' he yelled into the rusty tube. Old Barnacle listened for a moment.

"ELLO!' the old troll wheezed back. 'WHAT D'YA WANT?'

'WE'RE POPPIN' OFF TO VISIT THE CLUNK . . . TO SEE LADY JAUNDICE,' Clod yelled.

A flash of recognition passed across Old Barnacle's weathered face.

'LADY JAUNDICE?' the old troll croaked. 'YOU'RE VISITIN' THE TROLL THAT STOLE?'

'YES!' Rubella snapped impatiently.

'S'RIGHT!' said Clod. 'WE NEED A RIDE IN YOUR BOAT.'

'OH . . .' Old Barnacle wriggled down from Rubella's shoulder and smiled at everyone. He was naked except for a pair of tatty red-and-white-striped trousers. There was a tattoo of an anchor on his shoulder and another on his forearm that said Mooma. 'WHY DIDN'T YOU SAY SO?'

Neville tiptoed to the edge of the dock and looked down at the rusted tin boat that bobbed up and down below.

'Is it safe?' Neville said into Old Barnacle's ear trumpet.

'SAFE?' Old Barnacle laughed. 'THERE AIN'T NO SAFER BOAT THAN THIS'UN. LET ME INTRODUCE YOU . . . EVERYONE, THIS IS *OLE SINKY*!'

Meanwhile

Somewhere far below the surface of the Undersea, something gigantic stirred, flexed its fins and opened one gargantuan eye. It stayed there for a moment or two before suddenly, with a thrash of its tail, heading off through the crushing blackness. It had been asleep for a very long time and it was very, very hungry.

Across the Undersea

Neville's stomach heaved as the little boat rolled over the crest of a high wave. Its ancient engine rattled and spluttered, steaming like a kettle.

How had this happened? How was Neville in the middle of a pitch-dark ocean, squished between his mooma and dooda, on the way to visit his grandma Joan in prison? He looked up at the Clunk glowing in the distance and shuddered.

'Dooda? D'you think Grandma Joan is all right in there?' Neville asked. 'I mean . . . Lady Jaundice. D'you think she's OK?'

'Oh, don't you fuss about ole Jaundice,' said Clod. 'She's tough as a tinker's toenails. And, anywho, the old gonker deserves everythin' she gets.'

'That she does, my lump,' Malaria joined in. 'Jaundice was a right pain in the poodley-parts, if you don't mind me sayin'. Ain't that right, Pong?'

'Oooooorhhh!' cooed Pong excitedly. He was sitting right on the very bow of the boat like a tiny troll-figurehead. Neville looked at Pong and felt a little bit jealous. Despite adventures that included defeating a slurch and trapping a troll-criminal, Neville was still scared, but Pong seemed to be lapping it up.

'SQUALLS AHEAD!' wheezed Old Barnacle from his place at the wheel. His long beard streamed out behind him as they went. 'HOLD ON!'

'Right you are, Old Barnacle.' Clod beamed like an excited troll-sized puppy at feeding time. 'Oh, Nev, the Clunk is a right spine-jangler of a place. It'll judder your giblets, it will. I had a chumly that visited once and his toadstools turned grey from so much grunty-groaning.'

Neville's heart started to race. He felt the way he had on his very first visit to the Underneath, the night that Pong climbed up the toilet and Clod had accidentally snatched him instead.

'Stop scarin' him, Clod,' said Malaria. She elbowed Clod in the ribs. 'The poor lump looks yelpish.'

Malaria was right. Neville tried to give a little laugh as if to say, *Me? Scared? Don't be silly*, but he was. His heart was pounding against his ribs and the hairs on the back of his neck were tingling.

He peered into the gloom and shuddered. Now and again, a solitary buoy would float past with a jam-jar lantern on top and illuminate the swollen purple waves. It made him feel as small and helpless as an ant in the middle of a puddle.

'Don't fall in, Nev,' hissed Rubella. She gave Neville a shove to scare him.

'I'm not going to,' Neville said through gritted teeth. He was determined not to look afraid in front of his fat gonk of a sister. 'And, anyway, I can swim . . . sort of.'

Rubella's face spread into a sneer. 'It ain't the swimmin' you need to worry about, you snot. It's what's down there.' She pointed at the water with a sausage finger.

'Yes, I know,' Neville snapped, trying not to think about it.

'Don't forget, there's all sorts of nasties lurkin' about the Undersea,' she said. 'Monsters!' Rubella fished inside the pocket of her filthy dress and pulled out a half-eaten chunk of whatever revolting thing she'd been snacking on. Neville didn't like this one bit. She had that look in her eye, like the time she'd tried to get him eaten by slurches or the time she'd stolen Herbert's car and smashed it to pieces.

'What you up to, Belly?' Clod asked over her shoulder.

'Nothin',' Rubella replied, sighing cheerfully. 'Just showin' Nev the wildlife.'

With that, Rubella tossed the chunk of food into the water and everyone watched it bob away from the boat. Even Pong stopped cooing for a moment and looked.

'Nothing's happening,' said Neville. He wasn't sure why, but he was whispering.

'SSSHHHHH!' hissed Rubella, smacking a grubby hand over Neville's mouth. 'Watch.'

Just when it looked like the food-chunk was about to float out of the reach of the lantern light, there was a deafening roar, followed by a massive eruption of water. Suddenly a shrimp the size of a bus emerged from below the surface like something from a horror film. Its mammoth pink jaws were twice as long as the boat and they clashed like boulders smashing together. Neville screamed and toppled backwards into Malaria's lap.

In an instant the massive thing crashed back into the water, sending a huge wave right over the little boat, filling it with sea creatures and drenching everyone.

'Ha ha!' Clod shouted. He poked at the squid that had landed in his lap and laughed. 'It's all squidgerous.'

'How jiggish,' Malaria beamed, picking a flapping eel from round her feet and tossing it overboard. 'Do it again, Belly.'

'NOOOO!' Neville shrieked. He sat back up with his hair soaked flat over his eyes. '*What was that thing?*'

Malaria shrugged. 'Just a tiddler. 'Ere, where's Belly?'

Neville looked round the boat and almost fainted. His sister was gone.

'Oh, pook,' said Clod. He leaned over the edge of the boat and looked down into the water. 'RUBELLA?'

'BELLY!' Malaria screamed as she yanked at a starfish that had stuck to her shoulder.

'She must have been washed over.' Neville's heart leapt into his throat. He was just contemplating diving in to search for his stupid sister when –

'AAAAAAAAAGGHHH!'

The voice came from somewhere above and was muffled, like someone shouting on the inside of a balloon. Neville looked up and gasped. Pong pointed with a huge grin on his face.

'FOUND HER!' Old Barnacle laughed. His beard was flapping, alive with little fish.

Neville had seen a lot of strange things in the past, but he'd never

41

seen a troll-girl clinging to the top
of a boat's mast with an octopus
suckered to her face.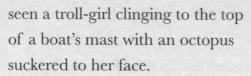

'Oh, Belly, you nogginknocker,'
Malaria chuckled.

''Ere's me thinkin' you've gone
overboard and all along you just
wanted a better view,' said Clod.
'I'd 'ave joined you if I'd known.'

'GEHH IHH OHH!' Rubella yelled from
behind the thing clinging to her head.
'QUIHH!'

'Ooopsy,' Malaria said. She pulled Rubella
down from the mast and tugged at the octopus
with both her hands. 'Clingly little pesters,
ain't they?'

'IHH WANHH TOHH GOHH HOHH!'

Rubella sobbed. 'AAAAAGGHH!'

'Hold still, Belly,' said Malaria. She gave the creature one last enormous yank and it came away with an elastic-sounding *SNAP* as Pong clapped wildly.

Suddenly free from the octopus's grip, Rubella launched herself at Neville. 'THAT WAS YOUR FAULT!' she blubbed. 'YOU DUNGLE DROPPING!'

Neville almost forgot his fear and burst out laughing. There were little sucker marks dotted all over Rubella's face.

'I want to go home,' the fat troll-girl snorted.

'AIN'T NO GOIN' BACK NOW,' said Old Barnacle. 'ONLY FORWARD.'

'Don't you tell me what I can and can't do,' Rubella snapped.

'Well, Nev,' said Clod, laughing, 'now you've seen a real-life Undersea monster.'

'THAT WEREN'T NO MONSTER,' Old Barnacle said, lighting up a clay pipe and puffing big smoke rings out over the water. 'THAT WERE A WEE NIPSTER. JUST A PLUGLET, REALLY. ABSOBLUNKIN' TEENSY.'

'A nipster?' Neville asked. 'You mean there're *bigger* things down there?' He looked out over the gloom and felt his stomach squelch sickeningly. Rubella burst out crying.

'YES, INDEEDY,' said Old Barnacle with a grim expression. 'MUCH BIGGER AND MUCH HUNGRIER.' He then yanked a big bottle of dark green liquid out from behind the rudder. 'WHO'S FOR A SWIGGLE OF FROG GROG?'

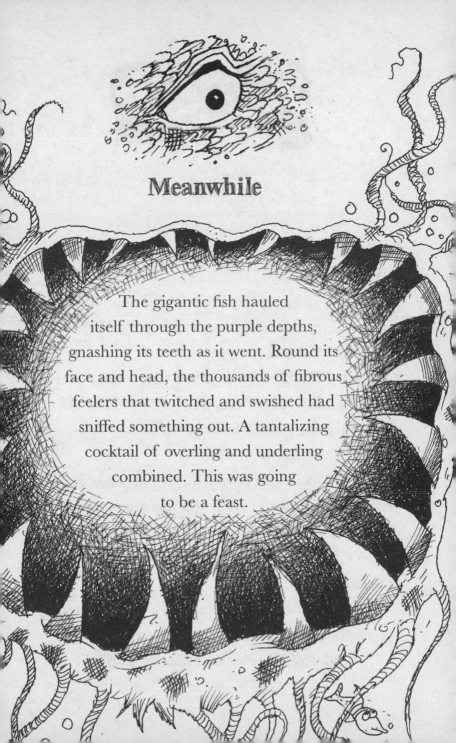

Meanwhile

The gigantic fish hauled
itself through the purple depths,
gnashing its teeth as it went. Round its
face and head, the thousands of fibrous
feelers that twitched and swished had
sniffed something out. A tantalizing
cocktail of overling and underling
combined. This was going
to be a feast.

Grunched

'Good gracicles,' said Clod, leaning in excitedly. 'What else?'

Neville stared at his dooda and wished he would stop asking questions. How much longer before they got to dry land?

'ALL THOSE GROTTISH CRUMPS AND CREAKERS AIN'T NEARLY AS BADLY AS . . .' Old Barnacle paused for a moment.

'As what?' asked Neville.

'AS . . .' said Old Barnacle. He was enjoying telling his sea stories a little bit too much. 'AS THE MOST POOKIN'LY TERRORSOME THING THAT EVER SWAM IN THE GREAT DOOKY DEEP.'

Neville could barely breathe. He leaned forward on the bench. 'What's that?' he whispered.

'GUNDISKUMPS!' Old Barnacle yelled,

brandishing his ear trumpet like a cutlass. 'AS BIG AS A MOUNTAIN AND MEANER THAN A MUNGLER.'

'What's a gundiskump?' said Neville, instantly wishing he hadn't asked.

'GUNDISKUMPS ARE THE BIGGEST OF ALL THE BIG'UNS,' said Old Barnacle. 'TERRIBLE THINGS; THEY SLEEP FOR HUNDREDS OF BANGS AND BONGS AND THEN WAKE UP HUNGRIER THAN A FATTY AT A TROLLABALOO.'

Neville listened with wide eyes and tried to ignore the fact that the butterflies in his belly had turned into eagles.

'AND THE MOST FAMOUS OF ALL THE GUNDISKUMPS IS GREAT GURTY. HUNGRIEST OF THE LOT, THAT ONE. IT'S FABLED HE'S GOT THE GREATEST TROLL TREASURE THERE EVER WAS STASHED AWAY IN HIS BELLY.'

'Junkish porkies!' said Malaria. 'There ain't no such thing.'

'IS TOO!' said Old Barnacle.

'Nonkumbumps,' Malaria chuckled. 'Don't you

listen, Nev. That's just a snizzly bedtime tale.'

'W-w-what do they look like?' Neville asked with a clenched bottom.

'ERM . . .' said Old Barnacle as he pointed to something in the distance behind Neville. 'WELL . . . LIKE THAT, REALLY.'

Neville spun round and froze. A mountainous beast was hurtling through the water towards them at tremendous speed.

'GUNDISKUMP!! QUICK!' yelled Old Barnacle. 'ALL HANDS A-ROWIN'!' He grabbed a set of oars from the side of the boat and flung one each to Clod and Rubella. 'WE'RE ALMOST THERE . . . ROW!'

Rubella started screaming and paddling on one side with all her might, making the boat go round in circles.

'C'mon, Clod!' Malaria bellowed. 'WE'LL BE GULPED!'

Clod finally started rowing and the boat began to pick up speed as he joined in with Rubella.

'It's not fast enough!' yelled Neville. 'We'll never outrun it!'

'JUST YOU WAIT,' Old Barnacle grunted. He

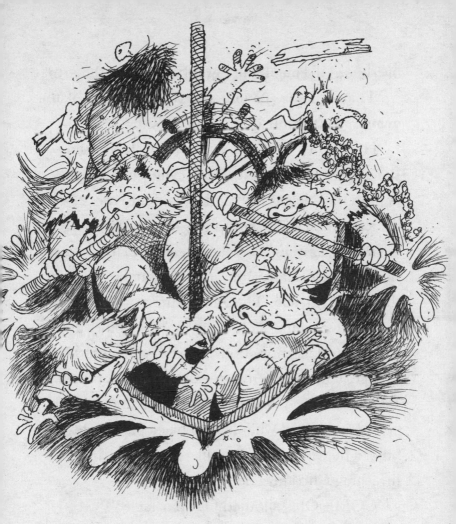

grabbed the bottle from the bench beside him and
emptied the last of the frog grog into the engine
tank. 'THAT OUGHT TO DO IT!'

There was a loud *BANG!* and the little boat tore
off towards the Clunk in a cloud of frog-grog-
smelling smoke. Neville would have toppled

overboard if Pong hadn't grabbed him by the arm.

'Thanks, Pong,' Neville yelled over the din of the engine. Pong grinned and cooed loudly.

'HOW'S IT LOOKIN', YOUNG'UN?' Old Barnacle shouted to Neville. Neville clambered behind the ancient troll and looked into the distance. The gundiskump was much closer.

'*It's gaining on us!*' Neville screamed. He could see the great fish clearly now and he thought he might throw up with fear. The gundiskump was the size of a shopping centre – a hulking mass of spines and scales – and its entire body glowed with a ghostly orange light. Between its massive eyes sprouted a spine as long as Neville's back garden and from the end of it dangled what looked like a giant light bulb. The whole thing was like some monstrous, thrashing Christmas decoration.

'COME ON!' shouted Old Barnacle. 'PUT YOUR BACKS INTO IT!'

Neville looked about at the chaos. This was a nightmare. Clod and Rubella were rowing up a storm, splashing water high into the darkness on either side of the boat, and Malaria was tearing big chunks of wood from the benches and throwing them at the fish as it approached. Neville watched as a huge piece bounced off the gundiskump's scaly forehead. It was like throwing peas at an elephant.

'WE'RE ALL DOOMED!' Rubella suddenly screeched. 'I DIDN'T EVEN WANT TO SEE YOUR STUPID GRANDMOOMA!!'

'*GGRRAAAAAAAAAAAAAAAAAAAAAAAA!!!*' the fish roared as it tore through the waves. It was so close Neville could smell its hot breath as a huge gust hit him.

'QUICK!' Old Barnacle shouted. He spun the wheel and tried to change direction, but it was too late. The gundiskump had caught up with them. Using its giant light bulb like the wrecking ball on a crane, it *thwack*ed the little boat high into the air.

'SAY YOUR GOODBYES!' Old Barnacle wailed as he flew out of sight, the wheel still clutched firmly in his hands. 'ALL'S LOST!'

'OH, POOK!' bellowed Clod. 'THIS IS IT!'

Neville shot upwards into the darkness. All around he could see his troll-family tumbling and clawing at the air as *Ole Sinky* splintered into little pieces with a sickening crunch.

Below, the nightmare fish snarled as it waited for

dinner to fall
back down
into its jaws.

'NEV!'
Suddenly a
hand grabbed hold
of Neville's. He looked
back and saw Rubella. He'd
never seen her looking so
afraid. 'HANG ON!' she
screamed. 'JUST HANG ON!'

Everything seemed to be moving in slow motion.
Neville looked down into the gaping black maw of
the gundiskump. He watched as Clod, Malaria and
Pong fell one by one towards the enormous mouth.

'OH, POOK!' shouted Clod.

'AAAAAAAGH!' bellowed Malaria.

'OOOOOOOOORHHH!' cooed Pong.

Here goes, Neville thought, screwing his eyes shut.
*The gundiskump has eaten my parents and now it's going to
eat me. I'm fish food.*

'Swim, Nev!'

CCRRAAAAAASSHH!

At the moment Neville thought the gundiskump was going to grind him into Neville-marmalade with its massive fangs, it clamped its jaws shut. Neville and Rubella hit the wall of teeth with a painful *wallop* and instantly bounced back off.

'DON'T LET GO!' Rubella screamed as she gripped hold of Neville.

Neville landed with a *SPLOOSH* in the freezing ocean. He barely had time to splutter and catch his breath before –

'LOOK OUT!' Rubella yanked his arm and pointed upwards. The gundiskump was flopping back into the waves and was about to land on top of them.

'SWIM, RUBELLA . . . SWIM!' Neville yelled.

'I AM SWIMMIN'!' she yelled back.

Neville's legs were numb from the icy water. He pushed and kicked as hard as he could, but he didn't seem to be going anywhere. This was the end. His arms were getting tired and try as he might, Neville couldn't make them work. How was he supposed to outswim a sea monster?

'DON'T STOP NOW, YOU DONKER!'

Rubella grabbed Neville and swung him on to her back. Just as he was about to give up hope, a wave as big as a house shot out from beneath the great fish and carried them off, spluttering and gurgling.

Neville, clinging on to Rubella's turnips and riding on her shoulders, watched as the gundiskump vanished beneath the waves with one final explosion of water.

'*MOOMA! DOODA!*' Neville cried. 'NOOOO!'

The glowing monster became a wobbly shimmer as it sank further and further below them.

'AAAAAAGGHH!' Rubella sobbed. She grabbed hold of a chunk of *Ole Sinky*'s hull as it rushed past on the current. '*What are we goin' to do?*'

Neville couldn't speak. He'd never seen his sister in such a howling mess before. 'I . . . I . . . um . . .'

The reality of what had just happened hit him like a fist in the stomach. The gundiskump was gone, and with it his troll-parents and his little brother.

'THIS IS YOUR FAULT!' Rubella screamed as she hauled herself up out of the water. 'ALL BECAUSE WE HAD TO GO AND SEE YOUR BLUNKIN' GRANDMOOMA.'

'What *are* we going to do?' Neville echoed Rubella's question with a whimper. Tears started pouring down his cheeks.

'I don't know.'

'I can't even remember which way we came from.'

'Just shut up and let me think,' Rubella snapped. 'I –'

Suddenly a large bubble erupted on the surface of the water right next to them.

GLUG . . . BLUB . . . PLOB . . . GLUG

Neville looked down and started to shake.

'Is it coming back?' he asked through chattering teeth.

Another bubble appeared . . . then another . . . and another. The gundiskump was returning to collect the remains of its dinner.

GLUG . . . BLUG . . . BOB . . . BOB . . . CHUG

The bubbles were getting bigger and bigger.

'Nev . . .' Rubella took hold of Neville's hand. In the light from a passing buoy, Neville watched an odd expression settle on his troll-sister's face.

'Are you all right?' he asked.

Rubella's mouth twitched, then her eyes widened and from her lips came the most shocking words Neville had ever heard. 'If we're goin' to die, there's somethin' I want to say before we go.'

'What?' said Neville, bracing himself. What was she going to say? Surely Rubella wasn't going to say something kind, was she?

'Well . . .' said Rubella.

'Yes?'

'I HATE YOU!!!!' Rubella screeched.

SPLOOOOOOSH! Old Barnacle bobbed to the surface in a flurry of yet more bubbles. 'WELL, THAT WERE UNEXPECTABLE.'

Rubella looked like she'd just been slapped round the face. She gawped at the old troll, then turned to Neville and shoved him into the water. '*Guh!*' she screamed. '*Ugh!* I thought we were about to die!'

'WHAT A PICKLE,' Old Barnacle huffed as he swam over.

'We thought you were the monster,' Neville spluttered as he struggled back on to the chunk of *Ole Sinky* for the second time.

'WHO?' said Old Barnacle. He raised his ear trumpet. How he'd managed to hold on to it, Neville couldn't even begin to guess.

'What do we do now?' said Rubella. She waited for Neville to get completely out of the water before pushing him back in again.

'THAT'S EASY,' said Old Barnacle. He reached *Ole Sinky*, but didn't climb up. Instead, he helped Neville on, then grabbed hold of the side and started kicking his ancient legs, propelling the boat through the water. 'WE'LL GO SEE OLE JAUNDICE, OF COURSE. SHE'LL KNOW WHAT TO DO!'

'WHAT?' Neville shouted so Old Barnacle could hear. Tears welled up in his eyes again. 'WHAT'S THE USE? EVERYONE'S GONE.'

'SO LET'S GET 'EM BACK.'

'How?' A tingle of hope sparked to life in Neville's belly.

'WITH A GOBBER THAT BIG, A GUNDISKUMP NEVER BOTHERS TO CHEW. YOUR FOLKS'LL BE FINE AND DANDY IN GREAT GURTY'S BELLY.'

'Great Gurty?' said Rubella.

'THAT WEREN'T JUST ANY OLD GUNDISKUMP,' Old Barnacle grunted. 'I'D RECOGNIZE THOSE GNASHERS ANYWHERES. THAT WAS GREAT GURTY AN' NO MISTAKIN'. IF YOU WANT YOUR MOOMA AND DOODA BACK, IT'S LADY JAUNDICE WHO'LL KNOW HOW TO GET 'EM. WE'LL HAVE TO BE QUICK, THOUGH. IF GREAT GURTY GOES BACK TO SLEEP AT THE BOTTOM OF THE UNDERSEA, THEY'LL BE STUCK DOWN THERE FOREVER.'

'But Jaundice is still behind bars,' Neville said, cupping his hands like a loudspeaker.

'WELL, WE'LL JUST HAVE TO THINK OF SOMETHIN' WHEN WE GET THERE,' said Old Barnacle.

Meanwhile

Somewhere deep in the belly of Great Gurty, Malaria rolled over and opened one eye. Something was very wrong. Everything was pitch-dark and a strange gurgling sound was echoing all around her.

'Hello?' she called, trying to figure out why she was soaked through and her head felt like it had been smashed between two big cymbals. 'CLOD?'

In the blackness, the sound of a pair of heavy feet slapped their way towards her.

''Ello, my brandyburp!' beamed Clod's voice. 'We thought we'd lost you. SHE'S OVER 'ERE!'

Suddenly a light flared up from round a corner and Pong bounded into view, carrying a lantern made from a jar filled with tiny glowing plankton.

'Squibbly.' Clod chuckled. 'That's everyone then. Seems like Rubella and Nev had a luckly escape.'

Malaria scrambled to her feet and looked around

the enormous cavern of fish stomach. 'Who's
'ungry?' she said, rolling up her sleeves. 'No better
place than a gundiskump's gut to rustle up some
food. Let's go and see what else he's eaten.'

With that, Clod, Malaria and Pong lumbered off
into the darkness, licking their lips and humming to
themselves.

The Clunk

'What now?' asked Neville, barely able to speak. He was still trying to catch his breath after climbing up the hundreds of rocky steps from the beach below.

'How should I know, you squirmer?' Rubella huffed. She looked at Neville with a face like a pink, smacked bottom and scowled. She hated exercise. 'I don't know why I had to come all the way up 'ere . . . she's your blunkin' grandmooma.'

Neville didn't say anything. He watched as Rubella clomped off up the path, muttering to herself. This was all wrong. Beyond her, the Clunk loomed like something from an old black-and-white movie, soaring up and up into the gloom. It was a giant tower of iron girders and rusted rivets. At the top, like the lamp on a lighthouse, was a single cage, and in it a figure paced back and forth. Neville's heart jumped a beat in fear. He could hear his grandmooma bellowing from all the way down on the ground.

'Come on!' Rubella shouted over her shoulder. 'Stop being such a wimple.'

Neville didn't dare to argue. He followed closely behind his troll-sister as she plodded heavily along. It was like she didn't notice where they were. Neville glanced over the edge of the cliff path to the water far below. He could see Old Barnacle resting on top of a buoy among the rocks.

''ELLO!' the haggard troll shouted, waving. 'BRING ME BACK SOMETHIN' SQUIBBLY!'

Neville waved back and forced a smile. Something *squibbly*? What in earth was he going to find at the Clunk that was squibbly? He'd be lucky even to make it out alive, let alone bring back souvenirs.

Neville was concentrating so hard on not falling over the edge of the cliff and not bursting into tears or being sick with anxiousness that he hadn't noticed Rubella stopping. He walked straight into the back of her and nearly wedged himself right between her walrus-sized buttocks.

'GET OFF!' Rubella snapped.

'Sorry, Rubella.'
Neville wrenched
himself out from
between the
boulders. 'Yuck!'

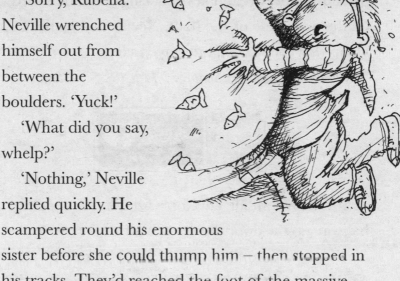

'What did you say,
whelp?'

'Nothing,' Neville
replied quickly. He
scampered round his enormous
sister before she could thump him – then stopped in
his tracks. They'd reached the foot of the massive
metal prison. Neville looked up and thought it
seemed like some kind of demented Eiffel Tower.

There was a neat, rusty building over to one side
with a sign by the door that said THE CLUNK PRISON
OFFICE.

Neville looked at Rubella, then back at the little
building.

'Right,' Rubella said. ''Ere goes.' She lumbered
over to the door, lifted the iron knocker and then let
it go with a swing of her chunky arm. It struck the
metal with a low, dull boom that shook the air and
rattled Neville's teeth. Almost instantly the sound of

bolts being drawn and keys clicking could be heard on the other side of the door. Neville and Rubella glanced at each other, but stayed silent.

Clunk . . . Click . . . Snap . . . Ti-ti-tick . . . Clack . . .

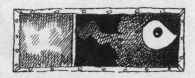

Suddenly a small, envelope-sized hatch about halfway up the door slid open with a *bang*. An eye the colour of pennies appeared and looked at Neville, then at Rubella. After having a good stare it slid upwards until there was a mouth showing instead.

'What?' said the mouth.

'Erm . . .' Neville fidgeted. 'Hello. I'm . . . um . . . I'm Neville Brisket and this –' Neville pointed at Rubella – 'is Rubella Bulch.'

'So?' said the mouth.

'We've come to see Lady Jaundice,' Neville whimpered.

'Tourist visitin' hours are over,' said the mouth. 'Come back tomorrow.'

'Oh,' Neville said, blushing. Rubella shoved him

towards the door. 'Sorry. You don't understand. I'm Neville Brisket – B-R-I-S-K-E-T. Lady Jaundice – The Troll That Stole – is my grandmooma.'

'Well, mangle my mushrumps,' said the mouth. 'I didn't realize it was you. We've been expectin' ya.'

With that, the little hatch slid shut and lots more bolts and chains and locks started clicking and clanking on the other side of the door. Then, with a gush of musty air, the door creaked open and a short, portly troll in a patchwork prison-guard's uniform waddled out into the torchlight.

''Ello,' the guard said, looking Neville up and down as if he was wondering what he tasted like. 'You've been the talk of the Clunk for yonks and yearlies, you 'ave.'

'Why?' said Rubella, scowling.

'Why?' laughed the prison guard. 'We heard ole Jaundice had waffled off and become an overling. When we found out that her nipster was comin' to pay her a visit, we all took bets on what you might look like.'

'Oh,' said Neville. 'And do I?'

'Do you what?'

'Do I look like you thought I would?'

'Well, it's hard to say,' said the guard. 'I was imageratin' you might be a lot taller . . . what with you overlings not havin' a ceilin'. Is it true you lay eggs?'

Rubella smacked her hand over the guard's mouth and leaned in close. 'We've had a bad day,' she growled. 'A VERY BAD DAY! Are you goin' to let us see Jaundice or aren't you?'

The prison guard peeled Rubella's stumpy fingers away from his face and frowned. 'Of course,' he said through gritted teeth. 'Where's my manners? I'm Bile . . . Prison Officer Bile. Come in and make yourself at home.'

'About blunkin' time,' Rubella huffed. She pushed past Bile and clomped in through the open door. 'Dungle droppings!'

Bile smirked at Neville for a second, then turned and followed Rubella, leaving Neville alone on the office front step.

Neville looked up one last time at the terrifying building that vanished into the darkness. Every little bone of his body told him not to go up there . . . but he had to. The Bulches were depending on him, and Lady Jaundice was the only one who might know how to get them out of the gundiskump.

'Think of Captain Brilliant,' Neville whispered to himself, then he took a deep breath and stepped inside.

Jaundice's Cell

The office was small and cramped and smelled of old books. All around were piles of yellowing papers, and the ceiling was covered in hundreds of hooks, from which dangled huge bunches of keys.

'Now then,' said Officer Bile, dragging a huge dusty book off a shelf. He hauled it on to an old desk and flicked through the pages. 'Sign your name here, please.'

Neville glanced at the empty entry in the book that Bile was pointing at and signed his name. Across the top of the page were the words *LADY JAUNDICE: THIEF, GONKER, TRUCCANEER – VERY DANGEROUS*. Neville gulped.

'We've got to go right to the top floor,' said Bile, closing the book and dumping it back on the shelf. 'Look lively.'

'What?' Rubella grunted. She still had beads of sweat trickling down her face from all the steps. 'I ain't climbin' any more stairs!'

'Not a problem,' said Bile, grabbing a bunch of keys from a hook and fastening them to his belt. 'We'll take the trollevator.'

Neville and Rubella looked at each other and frowned.

'This way,' Bile said. He led them out of the office and back along the path to the foot of the tower. 'I expect you've never been in a trollevator before.'

Neville shook his head and huddled close to Rubella as a line of grizzly guard-trolls tromped past with grim expressions.

'Well, there's a first time for everything,' Bile said. He unlocked a small gate in the barred wall and stepped inside. 'It's just in here.'

Neville stepped through and looked up in amazement. They had entered the huge circular tower. It was like staring straight up through a vast metal chimney. Round the outside of the room were row upon row and floor upon floor of guard stations stretching up and up as far as Neville could see. He couldn't spot any cells for prisoners at all.

'There are so many officers,' he said with wide eyes.

'Well, Jaundice is a right bad'un,' said Bile. 'We've got to make sure she don't get out.'

'And where are all the other prisoners?' Neville asked.

'There ain't any!' Bile replied. 'There ain't any other troll as terribonk as your grandmooma.'

Neville turned round slowly and took in the endless upward spiral of sentries and officers and heavies. There were faces peering down from all around and it made him feel nervous.

'Who's that?' shouted a voice. '*Bleuuch!* Overlings!'

'Oy, Bile,' shouted another. 'What you doin' lettin' tourists in at this time?'

Bile put his hand on Neville's shoulder. 'Take no

notice,' he said. 'Us guards get very bored standin' around all day.' Then he walked Neville and Rubella towards what looked like a big wicker basket dangling on a chain. Neville's heart started to quicken as he realized what he was looking at. The basket chain was attached to the highest girder far above.

''Ere we are,' said Bile as they reached it. 'The trollevator. In you get.' He patted the edge and smirked.

Both Neville and Rubella stopped and stared at the contraption. It looked like it might fall apart at any second.

Bile grinned at Rubella and winked. 'It's better than takin' the stairs.'

Rubella needed no more persuasion. In an instant she flopped herself over the edge and slumped head first into the trollevator. Neville watched her bulbous legs kicking in the air as she wriggled right-side-up. She reminded him of a boiled ham in a dress.

'Come on, Nev,' Rubella ordered. 'Stop being such a squirmer.'

Neville reluctantly clambered into the basket and

nestled in one of the corners. After nearly being eaten alive and drowned in one day, the trollevator couldn't be that bad, he supposed.

'Righty-ho,' said Bile. He pulled on a lever inside the basket and the grating of gears and whirring of cogs suddenly sprang into earshot from somewhere high overhead. 'To the top.'

The trollevator took off at great speed, twisting and jerking in mid-air as the chain was winched upwards. Neville watched as rows of angry-looking guards blurred past. His dooda was right, the Clunk was the most spookery place he'd ever seen.

'Almost there,' Bile shouted over the rushing and whirring.

They were so high, Neville didn't dare look down. The trollevator was now up among the rafters, whizzing past metal joists and steel beams at a frightening pace.

'I don't like this place,' Rubella mumbled in a low voice. Neville nodded to her in agreement.

'Let's ask Grandma Jaundice about the gundiskump and then get out of here,' Neville mumbled back.

There was an almighty jerk and the trollevator emerged out of the metal tower into the open air above. Neville looked down at the ocean far below and was very nearly sick.

''Ere we are,' Bile said and nimbly hopped out of the basket on to a narrow landing platform next to Jaundice's cell. 'This way, you two.'

Neville gingerly stepped on to the metal ledge and shuffled towards the cage, followed by Rubella.

Jaundice had smashed all the lanterns inside her cell, but Neville could already see what waited for him in the shadows.

'What now?' Rubella said as she reached Neville's side. 'Are we –' Then she saw it too.

Like a bad dream waiting in the dark, Neville could see the distinct copper glint of a pair of beady troll-eyes glaring at him. Then, in a voice like torn paper, came the words, 'Well, if it isn't my disgustin' snot of a grandson! Fancy seein' you here!'

'Hello, Grandma!'

'WHAT DO YOU WANT?' Jaundice bellowed from the shadows. A half-chewed bone from something she'd eaten for dinner flew through the bars and just missed Neville's head.

'That's enough of that!' Bile ordered in his best *I'm the leader around here* voice. 'Close your goblet.'

'Who are you?' Jaundice's voice cackled.

'Prison Officer Bile,' said Bile.

'Oh!' Jaundice snickered. 'I knocked the front teeth out of the last prison officer that told me to be quiet.'

Officer Bile gulped and took a step back towards the trollevator. 'Well, Neville,' he said. 'I suppose I should leave you to talk to your grandmooma.' Then he leaned in next to Neville's ear and whispered, 'Don't get too close to the bars.'

Neville nodded.

'I'm off to do my rounds of the other officers,' Bile said as he hopped back into the trollevator. 'Just give a yell when you're done.' With that, the basket disappeared below the landing platform, leaving Neville and Rubella alone at the top of the tower.

'Well?' came Jaundice's voice again. 'Aren't you goin' to come and say hello to your little ole grandmooma?'

Rubella walked over to the torch by the landing platform and took it down. Then she approached the bars. Neville gasped as the cell slowly filled with light. Lady Jaundice stood in the centre of the room, with the kind of smile on her face that a crocodile pulls just before it gobbles down its prey. The carrots on her shoulders and the twigs in her hair were massively overgrown

and sprouted through her striped prisoner uniform like an abandoned garden. She was like a walking salad.

'Hello, Grub,' she said, not taking her eyes away from Neville.

'Hello, Grandma,' Neville said. 'How've you been?'

'HOW DO YOU THINK I'VE BEEN?' Jaundice bellowed and ran at the bars. She banged them with her fists and growled like a wild animal. 'WHAT DO YOU WANT, YOU LITTLE FOOZLE FART?'

'Erm . . .' Neville said. He noticed Jaundice was still wearing her elbow-length gloves and pearls. Some things never change.

'Tell her,' Rubella whispered, nudging Neville. 'Tell her what happened.'

'TELL ME WHAT?'

'Well, Grandma . . . We need your help!'

Jaundice burst into fits of hysterical laughter. 'You want *me* to help *you*? You must be knocked in the noggin.'

'No, you don't understand,' Neville said, and ran right up to the bars of the cell. If his grandma

knew a way to get Clod and Malaria out of the
gundiskump, he had to make her listen.

'*WHAT* don't I understand?' Jaundice hissed,
pressing her pointy nose against Neville's.

'We were coming to visit you today because . . .
because . . . well, because you're the only person we
can turn to.'

'FAT CHANCE!' Jaundice screamed. 'I'd rather
eat a bogle's bumly bits than do somethin' for a slug
like you.' Jaundice looked up the hallway to the
landing platform, then back at Neville. 'Where's the
rest of you, anyway? It's been ages since I've made
anyone cry.'

'Well, that's just it,' Neville exclaimed. 'On our

way here, the boat got swallowed by a gundiskump . . . and Mooma and Dooda too.'

'AND PONG!' Rubella butted in. 'AND PONG!'

'Ha ha! I bet they tasted greasy,' Jaundice chuckled to herself.

'The old boat-troll said you might know a way to get them out. Please, Grandma Joan?'

Jaundice grabbed Neville by the collar of his sweater and lifted him into the air.

'Don't you *ever* call me by that name,' she barked. 'I AM LADY JAUNDICE!'

'OK,' Neville whimpered. 'Please, Lady Jaundice . . . you have to help us.'

'I MOST BLUNKIN' WELL DON'T HAVE TO HELP YOU!'

'Please.' Neville started to cry as he dangled in his grandma's hands.

'*EUUCH!* You're such a whelp,' Jaundice said. 'How did a grandson of mine turn out to be so nervish?'

'THAT'S ENOUGH! LISTEN TO ME, YOU PUFFLUMPIN', WRINKSOME, OLD GURNIP!' Rubella shouted.

Lady Jaundice dropped Neville to the ground

with a look of shock on her face. No one had ever stood up to her like that before.

'IF YOU DON'T TELL US HOW TO GET OUR MOOMA AND DOODA OUT OF GREAT GURTY, I'M GOING TO COME IN THERE AND –'

'*What* did you say?' Jaundice's face turned from shock to excitement.

'I said I'm going to come in there and –'

'No, no, no – before that. Did you say *Great Gurty*?' Jaundice asked.

'Yeah, why?' Rubella looked confused.

'Your folks were eaten by *Great Gurty*?'

'Yes,' Neville said, clambering back to his feet and wiping his eyes on the back of his sleeve.

'*I've changed my mind!*' Jaundice said. She looked like she was about to explode with excitement. 'I'll help you get your moomsie and doodsie.'

'You will?' said Neville. Something felt strange. 'Why?'

'They don't call me "Marauder of the Mud Beds" for nothing, boy! I LOVE a challenge!' Jaundice bellowed. 'Great Gurty is famous to us seafolk.'

'Tell us what we have to do,' Rubella said. 'How do we get them out?'

'Oh, no,' Jaundice said, crossing her spindly arms. 'There's a condition.'

'What?' said Neville.

'I won't tell you how to get your parents back, but I'll show you.'

'How?' asked Rubella.

'If you want to see your mooma and dooda again, you've got to break me out.'

'What?' Neville's heart sank. 'We can't break you out of prison.'

Jaundice leaned through the bars as close to Neville as she could get. A leer spread across her face like a rash. 'You scratch my warts and I'll scratch yours.'

Meanwhile

On the beach below the Clunk, at the foot of the cliffs, Old Barnacle clambered over the rocks. He wasn't as young as he used to be and cursed to himself as he stumbled on a giant clamshell.

When he reached the far edges of the rock pools, he stopped to catch his breath, then rummaged in his pockets and pulled out a small wooden whistle.

'This one's for you, Captain Jaundice,' he mumbled, then blew a long, high-pitched note across the water. 'It'll be squibbly to do some swashbunglin' again.'

Break Out

Prison Officer Bile was in the trollevator, swinging from guard post to guard post, when a loud rumpus started banging and echoing down the tower. He could hear shouting and screaming and all sorts of other horrible sounds. 'Oh, pook,' he grunted to himself, 'that was the overling's voice.'

Bile jammed the lever as far as it would go to take him to the top floor. 'Stay away from the bars! STAY AWAY!!'

As the chain clanked and jangled the basket up against the landing platform, he peered around nervously for signs of the little boy and his chublet of a sister. Where were they? The landing torch had been extinguished and everything was very dark.

'YOU'RE TOO LATE!' Jaundice cackled from inside her cell.

'What d'you mean?' Bile asked as he clambered

out of the trollevator. 'Where's that Neville?'

'They got too close to the bars,' Jaundice sneered. 'I ATE THEM.' Then she licked her lips with a sickening slurp.

'What?' said Bile. A look of horror spread across his face. 'How?'

'When you're as old as I am, you can chomp your way through *anythin'*,' Jaundice chuckled. Then she belched.

'Oh, I'm in trouble,' Bile whimpered, cradling his head in his hands. 'I can't have visitors being eaten on my watch. I'll never be head officer now!'

'Don't you worry,' said Jaundice with a knowing wink. 'I won't tell anyone. Who'd miss a lonely little overling, anyway?'

Bile thought for a moment. Maybe she had a point?

'I saved the best bit for last,' Jaundice teased. 'His little left sock.' She pointed to a small blue sock, discarded on the filthy floor just beyond her cell. 'In all the rambunkin' it flew through the bars and now I can't get it. *Please* don't take the left sock away, officer . . . *please*.'

A smile crept in at the corners of Bile's mouth as the deliciously stinky scent of left sock tingled his nostrils.

'I'm afraid I can't let you have that,' he said, trying to look official. 'I can't have you litterin' up the hallways with bits of overling. I'll have to take it away and . . . dispose of it.'

'OH NO!' Jaundice cried, dramatically slapping the back of her hand against her forehead. 'PLEASE!'

'No,' said Bile. 'I've made up my mind.' He turned his back on Jaundice and smirked. *Forget the boy, that sock is mine*, he thought. It was rare for such lummy tidbits to make their way into the prison.

'THAT SOCK BELONGS TO ME!' Jaundice screamed and started rattling the bars of her cell. 'HOW COULD YOU?'

'Shut up!' Bile ordered and stooped to pick it up, grunting as he went. His stumpy fingers just had time to wrap themselves round the woollen snack, when he caught a glimpse of ten chubby troll-toes poking out of the shadows just beyond it. Next to them was another pair of much smaller, pinker feet . . . one in a shoe, the other bare. 'What the –?'

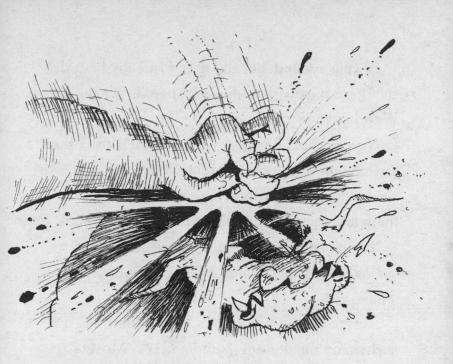

CRRRAAAAACCCKKK!!!

Rubella, concealed in a dark corner, brought her spade-sized fist down on the top of Bile's head with a *wallop*. The poor troll grunted loudly and fell to the floor, out cold.

'I'm not sure about this,' Neville said. He jumped out of his hiding-place and snatched his sock from Bile's limp hand. 'Doesn't this make us criminals?'

'Nonsense, m'boy,' Jaundice laughed. 'You'll make a fine truccaneer yet!'

'Yeah! *Clam up!*' Rubella snapped. 'You want to see Mooma and Dooda again, don't you?'

Neville nodded, but still didn't feel any better.

'Quick, Grub,' Jaundice whispered, 'get the keys. We don't have much time.'

Neville rolled Bile over on to his back and fished the big bunch of keys from the loop on his belt. He eyed them suspiciously. There were hundreds of them and they were all different shapes and sizes.

'I don't know which one,' Neville said.

'Well, get to it,' Jaundice barked. 'Start tryin' 'em.'

Neville started trying to fit the keys into the big keyhole on the door of Jaundice's cell. Most of them didn't go in at all and the ones that did wouldn't turn.

'Quick, Nev,' Rubella said, creeping to the edge of the landing platform. 'I can hear shoutin'. I think the other guards are on to us!'

Neville's heart was practically in his throat. He could hear it now too – the deep *TROMP* . . . *TROMP* . . . *TROMP* of marching troll-feet and raised voices.

'They're going to throw us in jail,' Neville snivelled.

'Not if you get me out,' Jaundice interrupted

impatiently. 'HURRY UP!'

Suddenly the trollevator jumped into motion.

'They've called it,' Rubella said, running back to Neville and Jaundice. 'The guards are on their way!'

'I'm going as fast as I can, Rubella.'

'Well, go *faster*,' Rubella snapped.

Neville picked a heavy, twisted key with a wiggly pattern up the side. 'Maybe this one,' he said. 'No.'

Then he tried a short stubby one with a silver handle. 'No,' Neville groaned hopelessly. Which one was it?

Finally, Neville picked a rusted key with a skull and crossbones carved into the end. He pushed it into the lock and twisted it . . . and the door swung ajar with a loud *click*.

'WELL DONE, NEV!' Jaundice yelled. She darted out of the cell, then wiggled her bottom and flapped her arms. 'Ugh, it feels good to have some space.'

'But what are we going to do?' Neville said. He could see the trollevator winch turning, which meant the guards were heading straight for the top floor. 'How are we going to get out?'

'Watch and learn, Nev.' Jaundice cackled wildly. Then she picked him up and swung him on to her shoulders.

'BUT –' Neville barely had time to think. What if Jaundice double-crossed them? He opened his mouth to protest just as Jaundice ran towards the landing platform and took a flying leap off the edge without a second's thought. Neville clung to her wrinkled neck so tightly he was worried he'd choke her, but he was too afraid to loosen his grip.

'*AAAAAAAAAAAAGH!*' Neville looked round as they fell and saw Rubella tumbling behind him. In the excitement, she'd jumped straight off the platform after them!

'HERE WE GO!' Jaundice screeched with delight. They were falling straight towards the trollevator that was now filled with brutish guards.

'THERE THEY ARE!'

'GET 'EM!'

'DON'T LET HER OUT OF YER SIGHT!'

Jaundice soared straight past the guard-filled basket and swung on the underside with Neville

flapping around her neck
like a human cape.

'THIS IS WHAT IT'S ALL
ABOUT!' she called over her
shoulder. Neville blubbed
in reply. *His grandma
was crazy!*

OOOOMF!

Suddenly the
trollevator jolted
and the guards above
all screamed in alarm.
Rubella had plummeted
straight into the basket and
landed on top of them. Neville
watched as one guard, then
another, then another, flew
from the basket and leapt to
the squish-free safety of the
spiral of sentry posts, howling
and cursing as they went.

'PULL THE LEVER!'
Jaundice shouted to Rubella
above. 'TAKE US DOWN!'

'RIGHT YOU ARE!' Rubella yelled back. The trollevator ground to a halt, then instantly started falling towards the floor below. '*AAAAAAGH!*'

Jaundice bounded free just before the trollevator hit the floor with a *crash*, but Rubella wasn't so quick. She lay in a daze among bits of broken basket and knotted chain. Jaundice grabbed her by the arm and hauled her to her feet.

'Come on, you porker!'

'*Oy*,' Rubella snapped, rubbing her boulder bottom. 'Who are you callin' porker?'

'NOT NOW!' Neville shouted. 'Look!' He pointed up the tower. The guards were all climbing down the walls and it wouldn't be long before they reached the ground.

'RUN!' Jaundice bellowed.

The *Rigor Mortis*

Jaundice burst straight through the metal gate, sending bits of lock and hinge flying in all directions.

'Ha ha!' she cackled. 'FREEDOM!'

Neville squeezed against his grandma's carrot shoulders as tightly as he could and closed his eyes.

'This is stupous,' Rubella huffed as she stumbled along behind. 'We're on an island . . . There's nowhere to go.'

'NONKUMBUMPS!' Jaundice shouted. She grabbed Rubella by the hand and pulled her down the hill, running faster and faster. 'The first rule of being a truccaneer is . . . NEVER GIVE UP!'

She started leaping down the steps, ten at a time.

'You've gone crooked in the clonker,' Rubella groaned, but Jaundice was ignoring her.

'BARNACLE?' Jaundice shouted. 'BARNACLE, WHERE ARE YOU?'

'What?' Neville said into his grandma's ear. 'How did you know Old Barnacle was down here?'

'The second rule of being a truccaneer is . . . know where your crew is at all times. *BARNACLE!*'

'WHO?' Old Barnacle came lumbering over the rocks, waving his ear trumpet. 'WHAT'S OCCURINATIN'?'

'OVER HERE!' Jaundice called.

'OH, IT'S YOU, CAPTAIN! I DID WHAT YOU TOLD ME TO, I DID.'

'What's going on?' said Neville. 'How do you two know each other?'

'This is Old Barnacle – first mate on the good ship *Rigor Mortis*,' Jaundice said. Old Barnacle saluted.

'I DID WHAT YOU SAID,' Old Barnacle mumbled like an excited schoolboy. 'AS SOON AS WE GOT 'ERE AND YOUR NIPSTER WENT IN LOOKIN' FOR YOU, I STOOD ON THEM THERE ROCKS AND SENT OUT A MESSAGE TO ALL THE CREW.'

'Good work, Barnacle,' Jaundice said. 'Now . . .

where's my ship?'

'WELL, IT'S JUST –'

'Hold on a minute,' Neville interrupted. He'd had about as much as he could bear. 'Are you telling me that this was all planned? You got our parents eaten by a fish so you could make us rescue your stupid captain?'

'Don't forget who his captain is,' Jaundice snapped, dumping Neville on the wet sand.

'YES, AND NO . . .' Old Barnacle said, grinning nervously. 'THE PLAN WAS TO BRING YOU LOT OUT 'ERE, LET YOU SEE LADY JAUNDICE AND THEN I'D SNEAK IN AND RESCUE HER MESELF. NO ONE PLANNED FOR THE GUNDISKUMP PART.'

'So all that stuff about savin' our mooma and dooda was all a load of grubberlumpin'?' Rubella said.

'A truccaneer never breaks her oath,' said Jaundice. 'You got me out of the Clunk, so I'll get your parents out of the gundiskump. A deal's a deal.'

Neville's head was swimming; this was all too much.

'First mate Barnacle,' Jaundice said in a leader-like way. 'Call my ship.'

'HA HA! INDEEDY, CAPTAIN!' Old Barnacle laughed. He pulled the whistle out of his pocket and blew it with all his might.

'What now?' said Neville.

'Watch,' said Jaundice.

Old Barnacle blew the whistle again. There was a moment of silence until . . .

HOOOOOOOOOONNNNNNNNKKKKKKKK!!

A ship's horn sounded a little way out to sea. Neville jumped and nearly screamed. All at once, hundreds of lanterns were lit and an enormous pirate ship flashed into view.

'Oh, my beauty!' Jaundice beamed. 'I've missed you.'

Neville couldn't believe his eyes. The ship had been moored so close and yet was completely hidden in the darkness. There were pirate-trolls all over the deck and swinging in the rigging, each one carrying a milk-bottle lantern.

'AHOY!' Jaundice shouted.

'AHOY, CAPTAIN!' came the reply.

Old Barnacle turned to Neville and gave

him a friendly nudge.

'HOW'S ABOUT THAT THEN?'

Meanwhile

'Mmmm, lummy!' beamed Clod. He was sitting
with Pong on the bank of a thin stream of water
that ran out of the darkness towards the
back of Great Gurty's gullet. In the putrid
water, bits of chewed-up fish and long
strands of seaweed bobbed slowly past.
'I've found din-dins!' he shouted.

Malaria watched in delight as
Clod and Pong started picking
things out like greedy diners in a
sushi restaurant. She sat next
to her family and pulled a big
globule of jellyfish from the
stream. 'Oh, lummy,' she
said, grinning. 'It's fresh!'

Roll Call

Neville stumbled up the gangplank with wobbly legs and butterflies in his tummy.

'Welcome aboard the *Rigor Mortis*, boy!' Jaundice laughed as he tripped and fell on to the deck. 'This is my ship, and this . . . is my crew.'

Neville looked up and saw a gaggle of troll-feet ahead of him. 'Be brave,' he told himself. 'You're the captain's grandson and no one is going to harm you.' He peeked a little higher and braced himself to meet the stare of hardened, scary, bloodthirsty . . . *Oh.*

'*Well?*' said Jaundice. 'Say ahoy to me crew!'

Neville stared at them. Lady Jaundice's pirate crew weren't quite what he had in mind. They were all as ancient as she was. Instead of cutlasses, most brandished walking sticks. One of them had a patch over both his eyes and another was even in a

troll-sized mobility chair with big wheels made out
of barrel lids.

'Ahoy,' Neville said in a small voice.

'WHAT?' said the troll in the chair. 'IS IT
BEDTIME?'

Neville said nothing and tried to hide his
disappointment. Scary pirates would have been bad
enough, but how were these old gurnips going to
rescue his parents?

Lady Jaundice placed one hand on Neville's
shoulder and the other on Rubella's as she clomped
up the gangplank behind him. Rubella caught sight
of the crew and burst out laughing.

'Ha ha!' she yelled.

'It's a truccaneer's life for you two . . . well, until
we get your family back,' Jaundice said. 'From now
on you'll be known as Blood-gulpin' Brisket,' she

said to Neville. 'And you,' Jaundice said to Rubella, 'will be known as Big-bottomed Belly.'

Rubella scowled at Jaundice, but said nothing. Even she was a bit scared of the old pirate captain.

'OK, YOU SEWER RATS,' Jaundice yelled over the crowd, 'IT'S TIME FOR ROLL CALL.'

A deckhand, with weeds growing where his eyebrows should be, shuffled forward and handed Jaundice a scroll of yellow paper. Jaundice unrolled it and started to read.

'Old Barnacle?'

'Ahoy!' Old Barnacle shouted, waving his ear trumpet.

'Blood-gulping Brisket? *BLOOD-GULPING BRISKET!*'

Rubella nudged Neville in the back. He jolted as he realized his grandma was talking about him.

'Erm . . . Ahoy!' Neville yelled.

'Big-bottomed Belly?'

'Ahoy!' Rubella grunted. She was not amused.

'Bilge, Spit and Blister?' Jaundice barked.

Three deckhands, including the one that had handed Jaundice the scroll, hobbled forward.

'Ahoy!' they croaked in unison.

'Rickety Spleen?'

'AHOY!'

'Mumps?'

'Ahoooooy!' cried the troll in the chair.

'No-eyed Ebola?'

'AHOY!' cried the pirate with two eye patches.

'Big Blurty?'

'*BLLUUUURRRGGGHHH!*' came the reply from a tall, skinny troll with his head lowered over a bucket.

'He never did find his sea legs, that one,' Lady Jaundice whispered to Neville.

'Poor thing,' Neville said. He didn't really know what else there was to say about a blurty troll.

'Canker?' Jaundice yelled.

A short, round troll, wearing an apron, stepped forward. Neville gasped when he saw him. Both Canker's hands were missing. Where his left hand should have been was a filthy old frying-pan,

100

and where his right should have been was a ladle.

'He must be the ship's cook,' Rubella whispered in Neville's ear.

'Ahoy!' Canker shouted and clanged the frying-pan and ladle together. Neville suddenly realized how hungry he was.

It had been ages since breakfast and even then he'd only eaten half his bowl of pickled fish eyes. He looked glumly out to sea and wondered if his parents were safe in the gundiskump.

'Squibbly,' said Jaundice, rolling up the scroll and tucking it away. 'We're off on an adventure, you rambunkin' rumpscallions. Set sail for the deepest part of the Undersea. We've got a gundiskump to catch!'

'RIGHT YOU ARE!' the crew all shouted together and dashed about, tying ropes and hauling sails.

Neville watched as the gnarled, grizzled crew clambered up and down the mast, unfurling Trolly Roger flags and singing as they went. Neville couldn't hear too clearly over the noise of the waves and the loud *click-crunch* of elderly troll-pirate joints, but their song went something like this.

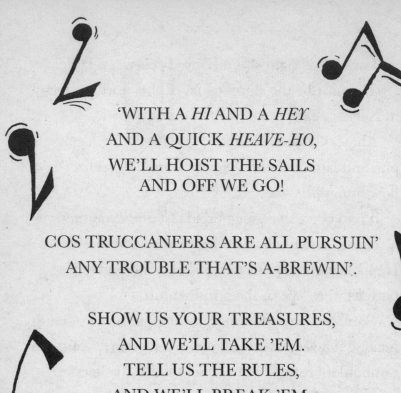

'WITH A *HI* AND A *HEY*
AND A QUICK *HEAVE-HO*,
WE'LL HOIST THE SAILS
AND OFF WE GO!

COS TRUCCANEERS ARE ALL PURSUIN'
ANY TROUBLE THAT'S A-BREWIN'.

SHOW US YOUR TREASURES,
AND WE'LL TAKE 'EM.
TELL US THE RULES,
AND WE'LL BREAK 'EM.
BOUNDERS, ROTTERS, GONKERS, WE,
SWASHBUNGLIN' BANDITS ON THE SEA!

WITH A *HI* AND A *HEY*
AND A QUICK *HEAVE-HO*,
WE'LL HOIST THE SAILS
AND OFF WE GO!'

Jobs

In no time at all, the *Rigor Mortis* was creaking calmly and rolling out over the bulbous, purple sea. Jaundice looked at Neville and Rubella as they stared into the darkness, and smiled. 'Don't you go worryin' your noggins off. I've got a score to settle with Great Gurty. We'll get him.'

'I hope so,' said Neville.

'I know so,' said Jaundice. 'But while you're onboard you'll work with the rest of us.'

'I'M NOT WORKIN',' said Rubella.

'Oh, yes, you are, chublin',' Jaundice said sternly. 'And, just for that, you can march straight off to the laundry. Plenty of panty-bloomers down there that need a-scrubbin'.'

'I AIN'T SCRUBBIN' NO PANTY-BLOOMERS!'

'THEN YOU WON'T EAT!' snapped Jaundice.

'*I hate you!*'

Rubella pulled a face like someone who had just swallowed a porcupine, and stomped down the stairs to the decks below.

Jaundice turned and looked at Neville. 'As for you, Blood-gulping Brisket, you can head off to the kitchen and help with dinner.' Then she turned to everyone else and screamed, 'SQUIBBLY SAILIN'!' and stormed off into her cabin.

Canker's Kitchen

Neville stood outside the door and listened. Inside, he could hear Canker banging pots and clinking his ladle. Maybe this wouldn't be so bad. At least he'd get to eat something, working in the kitchen. He opened the door slowly.

'Hello,' Neville said. 'Canker?'

'Well, if it ain't my overling assistant!' Canker shouted, his head half buried in a barrel of rotten fruit and vegetables. 'You took your time, littl'un.' He emerged holding a mangled orange peel in his ladle hand. 'Mmmmm, exotic.'

'Erm . . . I . . . uh . . . I'm supposed to help you with the cooking,' Neville said.

'Indeed you are, my trainee truccaneer, indeed you are.'

Neville stood in the doorway and stared. He wasn't sure what to do next.

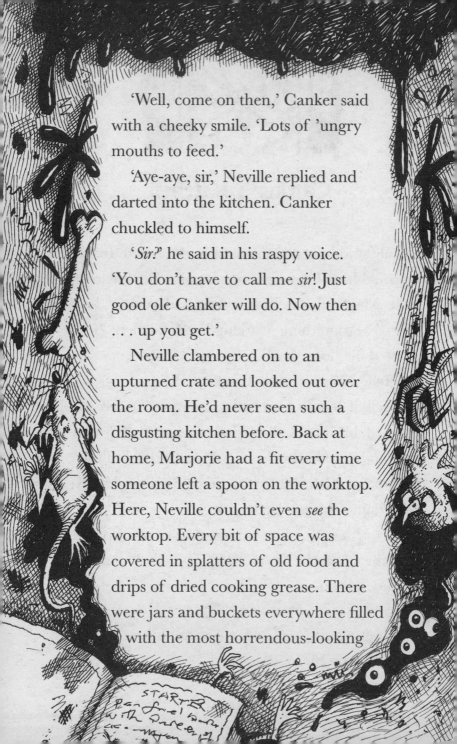

'Well, come on then,' Canker said with a cheeky smile. 'Lots of 'ungry mouths to feed.'

'Aye-aye, sir,' Neville replied and darted into the kitchen. Canker chuckled to himself.

'*Sir?*' he said in his raspy voice. 'You don't have to call me *sir*! Just good ole Canker will do. Now then . . . up you get.'

Neville clambered on to an upturned crate and looked out over the room. He'd never seen such a disgusting kitchen before. Back at home, Marjorie had a fit every time someone left a spoon on the worktop. Here, Neville couldn't even *see* the worktop. Every bit of space was covered in splatters of old food and drips of dried cooking grease. There were jars and buckets everywhere filled with the most horrendous-looking ingredients and the smell was unbearable.

At the far end of the worktop, nearest to Neville, was an open cookery book. It was like one of the books his mum kept on a shelf at home, only this one was covered in stains and wrinkly from getting wet too many times. Neville looked at the page and read aloud.

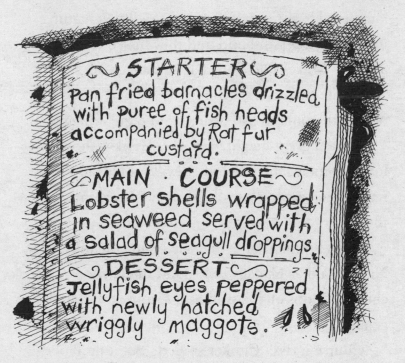

STARTER
Pan fried barnacles drizzled with puree of fish heads accompanied by Rat fur custard.

MAIN · COURSE
Lobster shells wrapped in seaweed served with a salad of seagull droppings

DESSERT
Jellyfish eyes peppered with newly hatched wriggly maggots.

'Sounds lummy, eh?' said Canker. He put his frying-pan hand over the stove and turned on the flame. 'Right then, what's first?'

Neville gulped and tried not to look too disgusted. He'd make sure he sneaked something a little less revolting when Canker wasn't looking.

'Erm . . .' said Neville, glancing through the recipe, 'it says fry the barnacles in a pan of sizzling hair-grease.'

'Ha ha, I love cookin' barnacles,' Canker laughed. He threw a ladleful of the little creatures into his frying-pan hand and they hissed and spat angrily. 'Makes Old Barnacle squirm, it does.'

Neville smiled a nervous smile. 'Then it says to drizzle the puréed fish heads from a great height.'

'From a great height? Um . . .' Canker thought for a moment, then, before Neville could stop him, he squirted a great arc of fish-head purée into the air.

'I don't think that's what the recipe meant,' Neville said as Canker ran round the kitchen catching globs of the stuff as it dripped off the ceiling.

'Course it did!' Canker smiled. 'So, little Blood-gulping Brisket, do you want to skin the rats or shall I?'

'You can,' Neville whimpered. He watched in

horror as Canker pulled the ladle hand off with his
teeth and replaced it with a blunt, rusted potato
peeler.

'There,' said Canker with a grin. 'That should
do the trick. Now . . . where did I put those rats?'

Nowhere to Sleep

By the time Neville had served dinner to the crew and Canker had licked all the pots and pans clean, it was extremely late.

'Good job, Blood-gulper,' Canker rasped, hanging up his apron on a hook by the door. 'S'pect you'll be snizzlin' off to your hammock soon, eh?'

'I don't have a hammock,' Neville said, close to tears with tiredness.

'Oh . . .' said Canker. 'Oh dear, indeedy.'

'Where am I going to sleep?'

'Well, there's plenty of kitchen cloths in the cupboard by the porthole. Never had any use for 'em myself, so you're welcome to sleep on 'em,' Canker said, yawning. 'If you get hungry in the night, grunch away, m'boy.'

Neville almost laughed. He was starving, but the only thing left over from the meal was the jar of fish-head purée. His appetite for troll-food had suddenly vanished, so Neville closed his eyes and thought of pepperoni pizza.

'Sleep tightly,' said Canker as he left him alone in the kitchen. 'Don't let the prawks nibble.'

Neville stood in the middle of the room and looked around; he had never felt so lonely. Shaking himself out of it, he headed to the cupboard by the porthole and opened the door. Inside were shelves of cracked plates and chipped mugs and – a-ha! – dishcloths. He pulled out a stack and arranged them into a pile on the floor.

'Oh well,' he said to himself, 'you're a truccaneer now. You'll just have to get used to it.'

Neville hunkered down and tried to make himself comfortable. He groaned. The dishcloths were rough and smelled like old food, and the rivets in the floor were sticking up through the pile.

'Oh, pook!' Neville whispered to himself. He wondered what Rubella was up to and realized he missed her. *Something is seriously wrong when you miss a hulking great bully like her*, Neville thought. He clambered back to his feet and headed for the door. He was sure he'd passed a whole row of cabins on

his way down to the kitchens earlier that day.
Maybe Rubella was in one of them now.

Neville opened the door a crack and peeked out.
The hallway was dark and silent. Suddenly the old
familiar butterflies returned to his belly.

He tiptoed into the darkness.

Lies . . . All Lies

Neville edged further along the hallway, stepping as quietly as possible. He could hear snoring coming from nearby and the sound of muttering.

'You should have seen it,' came a voice from the next room. Neville could see light spilling out from underneath the door. 'They believed me hook, line and dunker.'

Neville frowned. That was Grandma Jaundice's voice. He crept up to the door and pressed his eye to the keyhole. Inside, he spied Jaundice sitting at a table with Old Barnacle, Mumps and one or two other crew-members. Jaundice had changed out

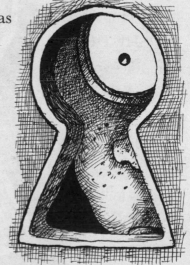

of her prison uniform and was now wearing a fancy troll-sized frock coat and thigh high, skrunt-skin boots. She even had a big hat with a weird-looking feather in it.

'Those little whelps actually think I'm goin' to save their family from Great Gurty!'

Neville's jaw dropped. That glumping old gonker had tricked them! What was he going to do? He wished he knew where Rubella was.

'WHATCHA GOT PLANNED THEN, CAPTAIN?' Old Barnacle yelled, gripping on to his ear trumpet.

'SHUT UP!' Jaundice snapped. 'Someone will hear you.'

'OH, SORRY!' Old Barnacle said just as loudly.

'Everyone knows the

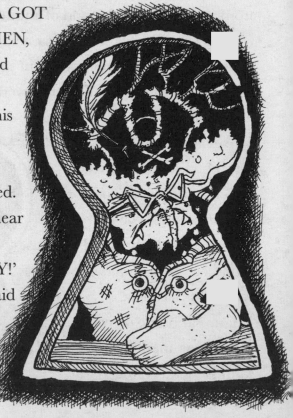

stories of the wondersome troll treasure that was buried in Gurty's belly,' said Jaundice. 'Years ago, Sir Arthritis III sailed a hoard of left socks into that honking great fish and no one has ever managed to get them out.'

'WHY NOT?' shouted Old Barnacle.

'Because Great Gurty is so lazy, only coming to the surface once in a blue mook.'

'Are you sayin' what I think you're sayin'?' said Mumps. He kept whizzing in and out of view as his chair shot across the cabin and back again with the rolling of the waves.

'That gundiskump will have a nice taste for overlings by now,' sneered Jaundice. 'I say we use the boy as bait to get Gurty to swallow us. Then, once we're inside, we dump Nev and the chunky sister with the rest of their family and sail out with the treasure. Agreed?'

'Agreed!' the others said in unison.

Waiting . . . Waiting . . . Waiting . . .

Neville didn't sleep that night, and he couldn't find Rubella.

The next morning he looked for the laundry room, but couldn't locate it. Over the next few days he tried to search the rest of the huge ship, but, being nearly constantly on duty in the kitchens, he didn't get much of a chance.

In the odd moments when Canker didn't need him to slice squid, pickle fish eyes or roast sea cucumbers, Neville would sneak off to the crow's nest at the top of the mast. He surveyed the decks from his vantage point, but still couldn't see Rubella.

While he was looking down, he picked at one of the toadstools that were sprouting across his neck and

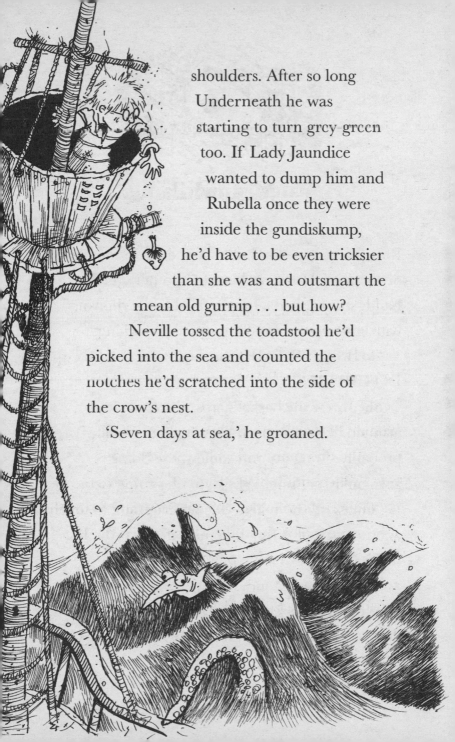

shoulders. After so long Underneath he was starting to turn grey-green too. If Lady Jaundice wanted to dump him and Rubella once they were inside the gundiskump, he'd have to be even tricksier than she was and outsmart the mean old gurnip . . . but how?

Neville tossed the toadstool he'd picked into the sea and counted the notches he'd scratched into the side of the crow's nest.

'Seven days at sea,' he groaned.

Meanwhile

Rubella sat in a cloud of steam, deep in the bowels of the *Rigor Mortis*, and howled. In her chubby hands she gripped a basket filled to overflowing with stinking truccaneer pants and stockings.

'THIS ISN'T FAIR!' she bellowed. 'I DON'T DO CHORES!'

She threw the basket across the room and grunted like an angry bull. Why her? Neville was probably sitting around somewhere doing absolunkly nothing! Why didn't he come to see her?

'That's it!' she yelled. She wasn't going to touch another pair of panty-bloomers if it was the last thing she –

Suddenly the laundry chute rumbled and hundreds of pairs of troll-sized underpants tumbled down on her head like an avalanche . . . a very smelly avalanche.

No More Waiting

HOOOOOOOONNNNKKKK!!!

Neville woke with dishcloths tangled round his arms and legs. What was that sound?

HOOOOOOOONNNNKKKK!!!

He sat up and looked around the kitchen. Canker was nowhere to be seen, so it must have been either very late or very, very early.

HOOOOOOOONNNNKKKK!!!

Suddenly the door burst open and in ran Canker, panting and banging his pan-ladle hands together.

'Quick!' Canker wheezed heavily.

Neville just stared. 'What?'

'Quickly, boy! *They've spotted Great Gurty!*'

Neville jumped out of his sleeping pile and ran to the door. He followed Canker along the corridor and up the stairs to the top deck, jumping two or three steps at a time. *This was it.* This was the

moment he'd finally have to outsmart Lady
Jaundice if he wanted to save himself and his
family.

Outside, crew-members
were running or wheeling
this way and that as
Jaundice stood on
the poop deck above
her cabin shouting
orders. She saw
Neville and smiled.
Neville scowled back.

'Ah, there you are,
my little truccaneer,'
she beamed. 'What did
Grandmooma promise?'

Neville felt like screaming,
*THAT YOU'D USE ME AS BAIT AND THEN
LEAVE ME INSIDE THAT THING!*, but he knew
he mustn't let on that he'd rumbled her secret.
Instead he just pulled a confused face and said,
'What, Grandma?'

'Look for yourself, boy.'

Neville ran to the ornate wooden railing and

looked out over the water. There in the distance was the unmistakable stalk with the giant light bulb on the end, rising out of the water. All round it the sea glowed orange as the gundiskump lurked just beneath the surface.

'Now all we have to do is get its attention!' Jaundice shouted over the hubbub.

All the hairs on the back of Neville's neck stood up.

He knew exactly what that meant.

Bait

Suddenly Neville didn't feel quite so sure about his plan. If he wanted to rescue his family, he had to go along with Jaundice's idea until they were inside Great Gurty.

'Now show me again,' Jaundice said, stroking her warty chin. Neville stood with a rubber tyre round his middle and wiggled like someone dancing the hula.

'Like this, Grandma?' Neville said, trying to sound as innocent as possible.

'Just like that,' Jaundice said with a sickening smile. 'You need to make sure Great Gurty can smell you in the water . . . are you ready?'

'Ready,' said Neville nervously.

'Go on then, boy!' Jaundice shouted. 'JUMP!'

Neville had no choice. He scrunched up his eyes, thought of his hero, Captain Brilliant, and leapt over the railing.

The water was icy cold and snatched his breath away as soon as he hit it.

'*AAAAGH!*' Neville screamed. 'It's freezing!' He tried desperately not to think about the fact that he was in the sea with all those monstrous things Old Barnacle had talked about. '*AAAAGH!*'

'Now, Nev,' Jaundice shouted over the side of the *Rigor Mortis*, 'WRIGGLE!'

Neville kicked and splashed anything he could move. He blew bubbles and jiggled his fingers and twisted his head this way and that.

'Is it working?' he shouted.

'Erm . . . NO!' Jaundice shouted back.

Neville twisted round to look for the light bulb on a stalk. It was still a long way off and didn't seem to be getting any closer.

'TRY AGAIN!' Jaundice yelled.

Neville tried again until it felt like his arms and legs were going to snap off.

'M-maybe G-Great G-Gurty isn't h-hungry?' Neville said through chattering teeth.

'Nonkumbumps!' replied Lady Jaundice. 'Gundiskumps are always hungry . . . Something's

not right.' The old lady thought for a moment. She
tossed her carrot stalks over her shoulders and
paced across the deck.

'G-Grandma,' Neville shivered. 'It's g-getting
very c-cold in here.'

'HOLD YOUR HONKERS,' Jaundice shouted.
'I'VE GOT IT!' Then she turned to her crew and
shouted. 'BRING OUT THE CHUBLET!'

A few moments later, Rubella was in the water
next to Neville with a tyre wedged round her
middle like a hairband round a hippopotamus.
Neville hadn't seen his troll-sister in ages . . . and
she looked awful.

'H-hello, R-Rubella,' Neville said, trying to smile. He desperately wanted to tell her about Jaundice's horrible plan, but knew Rubella would never be able to control her temper and go along with the old gonker, which would likely ruin their chances of getting Clod, Malaria and Pong back.

Rubella looked at Neville. Her face was filthy and her hair was even messier than normal. She opened her mouth and, for a moment, Neville thought she was going to yell at him, but she burst out crying instead.

'*They made me do chores!*' she wailed, with tears pouring down her face. 'I HAD TO . . . TO . . . WORK! *WAAAAAHH!*'

'It's O-OK, R-Rubella,' Neville comforted. 'We're almost th-there. They've found G-Great G-Gurty.'

'Wha?'

'Over th-there.' Neville nodded in the direction of the light-bulb stalk. 'S-see?'

Rubella craned her neck and looked.

'*AAAAGH!* NOT AGAIN!' she screamed and started thrashing and kicking in the water.

Jaundice ran to the railing. 'YOU TOO, NEV!'

she ordered. 'JUST LIKE BIG-BOTTOMED BELLY.'

'THAT'S NOT MY NAME, *JOAN!*' Rubella screamed.

No sooner had Neville started kicking his feet, he saw the light bulb start to approach at a tremendous speed. It raced through the waves, spraying water up on either side like a fountain.

'THAT'S IT!' Jaundice shouted. 'Gurty loves the taste of underling and overling together!'

Soon the light bulb started to rise higher and higher on its stalk. Then a scaly forehead the size of a football pitch emerged . . . then two massive eyes . . . then that terrible, enormous mouth . . . until Great Gurty's entire head was above the water.

It tore towards the ship at breakneck speed, spluttering and hissing.

Old Barnacle joined Jaundice at the railing.

'OPEN WIDE, YOU FUZZBONKIN' GREAT WHOMPER!' he yelled.

'IT'S WORKIN'!' Jaundice screeched. Neville could see that glint in her eye like the

time she almost destroyed the ticker-dinger-thinger. 'REEL 'EM IN!'

Bilge, Spit and Blister grabbed the ropes attached to Neville and Rubella's tyres and heaved them up on to the deck.

'BRACE YOURSELVES, SEWER RATS!' Jaundice bellowed over the din.

Neville just had time to clamber to his feet as Great Gurty's mountainous fangs passed round the ship. He watched as the mammoth set of jaws closed over them as if they were sailing into a tunnel.

Rubella grabbed hold of Neville's hand and whimpered as the teeth clamped shut and all the torches on deck blew out. There was an almighty, deafening *CRASH*, followed by an even more deafening silence.

'Well,' came Captain Jaundice's voice after a moment, 'we're in . . .'

Ahoy There!

Neville stood very still and listened as the crew of the *Rigor Mortis* stumbled this way and that in the darkness.

'OH, ROTSOME!' cried the voice of No-eyed Ebola. 'IT'S SO DARK!'

'But . . .' came another voice in the blackness, 'you can't see anyway – you're No-eyed Ebola!'

'Oh, yes . . . ha ha!' chuckled Ebola. 'I quite like it here.'

'MORE LIGHT!' came the voice of Jaundice. For a split second, Neville thought he saw her eyes flash a little way off. 'MAN THE LANTERNS!'

'AYE, AYE, CAPTAIN!' the crew yelled.

In no time at all, every milk bottle and jam jar was stacked on the bow of the ship and lit. Their glow became brighter and brighter as more and more were added to the pile, until the way ahead crept into view like something from a bad dream.

Neville looked about with eyes like dinner plates. They were floating in a lagoon surrounded by giant teeth. High above them, the roof of Great Gurty's mouth pulsed and squelched, and the occasional belch boomed up from a pitch-dark opening on the far side of the water.

'That's our headin',' Jaundice said, pointing into the gloom. 'Keep a sharp lookout, my truccaneers.'

'Yes, captain,' shouted No-eyed Ebola, walking straight into the mast.

I have to warn Rubella, thought Neville. If he didn't do it soon, it might be too late and Jaundice would throw them overboard or maroon them on a tonsil or something else just as bad. He sneaked round the back of a pile of frog-grog barrels.

'*Pssssssst!*'

Rubella, who had been wringing out her soggy dress and mumbling to herself, stopped what she was doing and looked in his direction.

'WHAT?' she yelled.

'*SSHHH!*' Neville hissed. Then he mouthed the words *Come here* in silence.

'NO!' Rubella growled. 'STOP WHISPERIN'!'

Before anyone could overhear his stupid troll-sister, Neville darted out, grabbed Rubella by the arm and yanked her behind the pile of barrels.

'What do you want?' she said, snatching her arm back.

'Rubella, I have to tell you something,' said Neville. 'Something terrible.'

'Well, go on then,' said Rubella. She stuck her fists on her hips and grimaced.

'It's all a trick,' said Neville urgently. 'Jaundice isn't going to save Mooma and Dooda!

'WHAT!!!'

'*Shhhh!* We can't let her know we're on to her . . . not yet.'

'What do you mean, she's not goin' to save them?'

'I heard her talking to the crew,' said Neville. 'She's after some treasure in Gurty's belly. She's going to leave us in here and make off with it.'

'That clonker!' Rubella grunted, rolling up her sleeves. 'I'll wallop her so hard, her bunions'll bounce.'

'No! You mustn't! *Not yet!*' Neville pleaded. 'We have to make sure we find everyone before

punishing her. Otherwise we might
not find them at all.'

Rubella put her finger
alongside her nose and
pulled a your-secret's-safe-
with-me face. Then she
winked at Neville and
marched back out on to the
open deck. Neville followed her
and headed to the railing to look out for his family.
He tried to appear as innocent as he could, but got
the feeling that all eyes were on him.

'KEEP HER STEADY!' Jaundice yelled from
the poop deck.

They were heading into the narrow passage at
the far end of the lagoon. Neville shivered at the
thought of it. They were actually about to sail into
the throat and down the gullet of a giant fish.
'*EEWWW!*'

'ULCER OFF THE PORT BOW!' Jaundice
shouted as they passed a huge fleshy lump sticking
out of the water. It was disgusting, like some
massive, meaty iceberg.

Neville groaned to himself and wished he were

back at home. He loved his troll-family very much, but he did always seem to get into terrible trouble whenever they were around.

The ship slowly rounded a bend in the throat and passed into another huge chamber. For a moment, Neville couldn't make anything out as his eyes adjusted to the darkness. But, as the lantern light filled the space, he saw . . . could it be? Neville almost tumbled overboard with excitement. In the distance, he could make out three figures huddled together on the far bank of the water.

'MOOMA!' Neville screamed with all his might. 'DOODA!'

He saw the figures jump at the sound of his voice and clamber to their feet. 'WE'VE COME TO GET YOU!' he shouted.

'NEVILLE!' echoed the sound of Malaria's voice.

'NEV?' shouted Clod. 'IS THAT YOU?'

''ELLO, LUMP!' Malaria yelled over the water. She started jumping up and down and waving. 'HE'S A BLUNKIN' HERO!'

Rubella rushed to the railing. 'WHAT ABOUT ME?' she barked.

Reunited

After a lot of tugging and pulling, the crew of the
Rigor Mortis finally managed to pull the Bulches
aboard in the baiting tyres.

'THIS IS A JUBBLY THING, INDEEDY!'
Clod shouted, clapping his hands.
He charged across the deck,
lifted Neville up and
planted a soggy kiss on
his head. 'I never
thought I'd see the likes
of you again, lump.'

'Dooda!' Neville said,
throwing his short arms
as far as they would go
round his dooda's neck.
'Is evcryone OK?'

'We're just fine and

bumbly,' said Malaria. 'Well . . . we are now that you're 'ere, Nev.'

'Well?' Clod said, stamping his foot. 'Where'd you get this rumbly old ship, Nev?'

'IT'S MINE!' a voice shouted.

Clod stopped talking and turned to the troll wearing truccaneer clothes, plus elbow-length gloves and a string of pearls round her wrinkly old chicken neck.

'You!' said Clod, pointing a stumpy finger.

'That's right!' Jaundice sneered, brandishing her cutlass. 'ME!'

The Betrayal

Jaundice's crew slowly closed in round Neville and his family, brandishing walking sticks and clubs made from bits of old scrap metal.

Neville gulped. *She can't betray us yet*, he thought. *I haven't even had time to tell Mooma and Dooda about Jaundice's plan.*

'Welcome aboard the *Rigor Mortis*,' the old gonker said with a sneer. 'Sadly, you won't be around to enjoy it for very long.'

'What you bramblin' on about?' Malaria said.

'SHUT UP!' Jaundice barked. She pulled out a second deadly-looking sword and bared her teeth. The light from all the jam-jar lanterns glinted in her pointy spectacles and made her look demonic.

'Please, Grandma Joan,' Neville said, stumbling forward.

'I'm *NOT* Joan!' Jaundice growled.

'But you promised,' Neville said. 'You promised you'd save the family.'

'*I did no such thing!*' Jaundice shrieked. 'I said if you broke me out of jail, I'd show you how to get your parents back. I've done that much.'

'But I helped you,' Neville pleaded.

'It ain't my fault if you two were stupid enough to assist the tricksiest truccaneer there ever was.'

'Oy,' grunted Rubella.

'And you can shut your rat-trap as well, you stonkin' great chunker!' Jaundice yelled at Rubella. 'I don't have time to stand and gossip with you bunch of worms. There's a treasure to collect in Great Gurty's belly.'

'Yes, but –'

'Yes, but nothin'! There's your rotsome little family,' said Jaundice, pointing at Clod and Malaria. 'I've repaid the favour of being broken out of jail . . . but I still haven't repaid the favour of BEING LOCKED UP IN THE FIRST PLACE! *CHARGE!*'

Fight!

All at once Jaundice's crew
hobbled into action. They
swung on ropes from the
yardarms and jumped down
from the poop deck like an
arthritic, crunching army.

'*Quick*,' Neville shouted to
Rubella. 'We've got to stop them!'

'Right you are,' Rubella said with a
huge grin on her face. She was obviously very
excited about a good brawl with a pack of
truccaneers. She rolled up her sleeves again
and leapt into the crowd, sending swashbunglers
flying in all directions.

'YOU'RE MINE, BOY!' Jaundice yelled and
stalked towards Neville. 'Think you can lock up
The Troll That Stole and get away with it?'

Neville yelped and darted into the throng of fighting trolls.

'TAKE THAT, YOU GURNIP!' Clod bellowed over the din. Neville turned just in time to see his dooda lift Blister the deckhand and toss him overboard. 'YOU LEAVE MY NEV ALONE!'

'*AAAAAAGGGHHH!*' Rubella had had enough and launched herself at Rickety Spleen. The troll-pirate stood there with a look of complete shock on his face as the troll-girl swung her fists and repeatedly boxed his head. 'I HATE TRUCCANEERS . . . AND I HATE THIS SHIP . . . AND I HATE GUNDI– . . . GRUNDISKIMPY . . . GUNDER– . . . I HATE GIANT FISH . . . AND I HATE-HATE-HATE YOU!'

Neville watched with a mixture of terror and delight.

The truccaneer battle was now raging all around him.

'THAT'S WHAT YOU GET FOR MESSIN' WITH A BULCH!' Malaria shouted, picking Spit and Bilge up at the same time and bowling them straight through the wall of Jaundice's cabin.

'Ha-haaaaaa!' Neville jumped aside as Mumps shot past in his chair. The old troll made a swipe for him, but missed and rolled straight through the open trap door to the decks below with a loud *CRASH*.

'WATCH OUT, NEV!' Rubella screamed as she booted Old Barnacle in the backside. Neville turned and saw No-eyed Ebola running in his direction with sharpened walking sticks in both hands.

'I know you're here somewhere,' Ebola yelled, running into the mast of the ship. 'Aha . . . there you are!' Then the blind troll started swinging and stabbing at the long column of wood with all his might. 'TAKE THAT, BLOOD-GULPING BRISKET . . . AND THAT!'

The scene before him was dizzying to take in. Neville ducked behind the pile of barrels and peeked out. He could see Lady Jaundice on the other side of the deck, stalking and sniffing the air.

'WHERE ARE YOU?' she bellowed. 'COME OUT AND FACE ME, YOU LITTLE FOOZLE FART!'

What was he going to do? Neville pressed himself as close to the barrels as he could and tried to think. They were on a boat. He couldn't hide from Lady Jaundice forever. He was going to have to face her . . .

Taking a deep breath and thinking of Captain Brilliant, Neville grabbed a discarded cutlass and stepped out from behind the barrels.

'I'm here, *JOAN!*' Neville screamed.

Everyone froze.

Lady Jaundice turned and faced Neville with a

look of utter rage on her face.

'*DON'T* call me Joan!' she bellowed and
ran towards him like a stampeding bull.
'*AAAAAGGGGHHHHH!*'

Neville quickly jumped on to No-eyed Ebola's
back.

'Wha's goin' on?' the troll
shouted as Neville shimmied past
his head and clambered up the
mast. If Jaundice was going to
grottle him, she'd have to catch
him first.

'*Out of my way!*' Jaundice
screamed, and shoved No-eyed
Ebola aside. She grabbed hold
of a rope that hung from the
yardarm and started scrambling
up the mast after Neville.
'COME BACK, BOY!'

'RUN, NEV!' Clod shouted
from the deck below.

'Push her off!' cried Rubella.

Not daring to look down,
Neville climbed as quickly as his

spindly arms would allow. He could hear Jaundice grunting just below him and expected to feel her sandpapery hand clutch his ankle at any moment.

'Keep going,' he huffed to himself. 'Don't give up!'

'YOU'VE NOWHERE TO GO!' Jaundice cackled from behind. 'I'VE GOT YOU NOW.'

Neville broke out in a cold sweat. His gonker of a grandma was right. He reached the yardarm and crawled out on to it. Below, Neville could see the upturned faces of his family and the truccaneer crew and he was so high up it made him feel sick.

'You're done for, snot stain,' Jaundice's voice whispered from right behind him.

Neville almost toppled off in surprise, but managed to regain his balance and then stood up, his feet and hands trembling wildly.

'PREPARE TO DIE, NEVILLE BRISKET!'

Neville turned and looked at Jaundice in all her terrible glory. She stood over him with her sword raised in the air and the glint of madness in her eyes.

'*GRAAAAAAAAAAAAAAA!*'

Pong clattered through the crowd and clambered

up the stairs to the poop deck. At the top, he waved to Neville, planted his little feet wide and started to swing something in circles above his head. Neville recognized it as his backpack. He'd dumped it on deck days ago and had completely forgotten about it.

'GO ON, PONG!' shouted Malaria. Then she turned to Clod and whispered, 'The poor lump's gone bunkers.'

'*OOOOOORRRRHHH!*' Pong cooed, then let go of Neville's backpack, which flew straight towards Jaundice's head. Everyone watched as the bag sailed through the air.

Neville suddenly had a flashback of hurling Clod's fishing-hook belt to trap Jaundice inside the ticker-dinger-thinger. Maybe . . . just maybe . . . the bag would hit her and send the old gonker tumbling into the –

THWACK!

Without even wobbling, Jaundice smacked Neville's backpack in a high arc across the lagoon like a tennis player smashing the ball. Everyone on the deck below sighed in disappointment.

'Ha ha!' Jaundice laughed. 'Pathetic.'

Neville watched sadly as the bag flew higher and higher as if in slow motion. He saw his mum's pack of baby-soft tissues fly out and fall forlornly into the water below. Then he saw the bottle of bleach tumble down, and the wet wipes, and a little tube of something blue – little tube of something blue? Marjorie's *Stink-be-gone* spray!

Before he even had time to hope that something might happen, the tiny spray-can hit the roof of Great Gurty's mouth and smashed into hundreds of pieces.

The Last Stand of Lady Jaundice

'*BLLLLLUUUUUUUUUUUUHHHHHHHHHHHH-HHHHHHH!!!*'

Great Gurty suddenly shook, sending a huge wave across the lagoon.

'Huh?' Jaundice wobbled and grabbed at the Trolly Roger to keep from falling. '*What's goin' on?*'

The *Rigor Mortis* lurched as another wave hit its side. Neville dropped to his knees and clung to the yardarm as tightly as he could.

'*What was that?*' Rubella shouted.

'Did we win?' mumbled No-Eyed Ebola to the mast.

Old Barnacle, who had been thrown to the back of the ship in the fight, suddenly jumped to his rickety feet and yelled 'SNEEZE AHOY!'

'*NOOOOOO!*' In an instant, Lady Jaundice forgot about killing Neville as panic spread across her papery face. She jumped down on deck in one great leap and landed with an almighty *crunch* of knees and ankles, and charged up the steps to the poop deck. 'MY TREASURE!'

Neville held his breath as Pong threw himself into Malaria's arms below. He half expected Grandma Jaundice to tear Pong into little underling nuggets, but instead, she ran and grabbed the ship's wheel.

'WE'LL BE BLURTED OUT WITHOUT THE LOOT!' Jaundice yelled to the remaining crew. 'QUICK! WE HAVE TO GET DEEPER DOWN THE GULLET!'

Deeper down the gullet? Neville jumped back to his feet.

'Dooda!' Neville shouted. 'Catch!'

'Yes, indeedy!' Clod beamed as Neville dived off the yardarm. '*Ooooommmfff!*' Clod caught Neville as easily as catching a soft ball.

'We have to get out of here!' Neville said.

'What about ole knuckly knickers?' said Malaria, pointing at Lady Jaundice.

The crew had already manned the oars and were heaving the *Rigor Mortis* towards the darkest part of the throat.

'The gonker's bungled in the bonce!' Rubella said, as she joined the rest of her family. 'If we go down into the belly, we'll never get out!'

'*Heave!*' Jaundice shouted to her crew. 'Come on, you swashbunglers . . . THINK OF THE TREASURE!'

'*BBLLLLLUUUUUUUUUUUGGGGHHHHH!!!*'

Great Gurty shook again. The wind had started to build up from somewhere above.

'We don't have long,' Neville said, jumping down from Clod's grip. 'Stop her!' He ran up the stairs to his grandma's side at the helm.

'KEEP GOIN'!' Jaundice screamed over all the noise.

Neville grabbed hold of Jaundice's arm and tugged. Her pearl bracelet snapped, then rattled all over the deck as the ship rolled back and forth.

'Grandma!' Neville said desperately. 'We'll all be killed!'

Jaundice wasn't listening. She didn't even notice Neville as he pulled and yanked at her stick-like arms. Her eyes were set forward like a rabbit caught in the headlights of a car and she muttered to herself continuously.

'Think of the glory, m'honks!' she boomed.

'*BBBLLUUUUUUUUUUUHHHHHHHHH!!!!!!!!!*'

There was an almighty *WHOOMF* and a wave higher than the crow's nest flared up at the far side of the lagoon. Neville saw it and felt his heart jump up into his throat. This was pointless. If they were going to escape, they had to do it without Lady Jaundice.

'Mooma, Dooda . . . *the lifeboats!*' Neville screamed. He tore down the steps, three at a time, and sprinted to his family's side. '*We have to get off the ship!*'

'You're the bossly, Nev,' Clod said and ran to the nearest rowing boat that dangled from ropes at the side of the ship. 'Everyone in!'

'*Ooooorrrrhhh!*' Pong sang with excitement. He stuck his tongue out at the approaching wave and laughed.

'Jump in,' Malaria called from her seat in the boat. 'Home's a-callin'.'

Neville was the last to clamber over the railing and flop into the lifeboat.

'We've got to cut the ropes,' he said, looking to his troll-family for assistance.

'Easy as stuffin' chunkers up a chimney,' Malaria said. 'Go on, Pong.'

Pong jumped up and bit through the rope in one great *CHOMP*. The boat wobbled as the ropes quickly unwound, then plummeted towards the water like a ride at the funfair. It hit the water and instantly bobbed away from the *Rigor Mortis* on the swelling current.

'This is it!' shouted Clod. 'Brace yourselves!'

The loudest *ROAR* Neville had ever heard sent the rickety little boat speeding back up the tunnels from whence it had come. Neville looked over his shoulder and saw his truccaneer grandmother, unwavering at the wheel, barking orders to her crew as her brambly hair flapped like the Trolly Roger in the wind and her pointy glasses winked in the lantern light.

WHOOOOOOOOOOOOOOOOOOOOOSSSHHH!

Back into the narrow passage between Great Gurty's throat and mouth they sped.

CRAAAAAAAAAAAAAAAAAAAAASSSHHH!

Past the mountainous mouth ulcer that was now almost completely submerged in water.

SPLAAAAAAAAAAAAAAAAAAAASSSHHH!

Straight across the lagoon surrounded by teeth and out between the tree-length chompers like a bullet.

Great Gurty had let rip the most belly-bungling

sneeze ever, spitting the Bulches and Neville high into the air. The monstrous creature gnashed its teeth at the darkness and was instantly gone back beneath the waves.

'Hold on!' shouted Clod as the lifeboat reached the top of its sneeze-propelled flight and started to fall back to the water below. '*Almost there!*'

Neville squeezed his eyes shut and held on to his dooda's arm as if it was a life vest.

Then, with one last *splash*, they hit the water. Neville opened his eyes, half expecting to see the boat splinter into hundreds of tiny pieces.

'We're out,' Rubella said in a trembling voice.

'Ha ha!' Malaria laughed, throwing Pong into the air and catching him again. 'WE DID IT!'

'*I* did it,' Rubella snapped, suddenly recovering from her shock.

Neville rubbed his eyes. 'What about Grandma Jaundice?'

'I think we've seen the last of that old gonker,' said Clod. He put an arm round Neville and hugged him close. 'There's no way she could have got out of that one. She was halfway down the gullet when that thing snoozled.'

'Now,' said Malaria. 'I don't suppose anyone has an oar lyin' about somewhere?'

Neville looked at his family . . .

His family looked at him . . .

Then all together they chorused . . .

'*AAAAAAAAAAAAAAAAAAAAGGGGHHHH!*'

Home

In the darkness of a Tuesday night, something wet slopped on to the tiles of the Brisket family's bathroom.

It was Neville.

'Mum!' Neville called, wriggling in the toilet water. He clambered to his feet and shook himself off. '*I'm home!*'

Herbert walked into the bathroom and stopped in his tracks. Then he stepped carefully towards Neville and gasped. Marjorie walked in and joined him. 'NEVILLE BRISKET, YOU'RE LATE!' she barked. 'You were only supposed to go down there for the weekend. It's been nearly two weeks! What about schoo–'

Marjorie's sour, little mouth suddenly dropped open as she gawped at the little grey-green child, covered in toadstools and stinking of fish guts.

'Well,' said Neville after a long moment, 'that was . . . fun.'

As if by clockwork, Herbert and Marjorie both fainted.

'Squibbly!' said Neville and lowered the toilet seat.

'Ello, grumplets. You've reached
the end of the book, you
brainy-bonkers, you. Now
that you're getting so goodly
at speaking trollish, here's a
few more words to add to those
whoppsy big brains of yours . . .

Absolunkly	Absolutely
Bumly bits	Your bottom
Chomplet	Bite
Clonktopus	A sea creature with a hundred arms
the Clunk	Lady Jaundice's prison

Delunktious	Delicious
Electric skrunts	Fish that can shock and fizzle you
Foobles	Stories

Frog grog	A truccaneer's favourite drink
Glugulars	Slimy sea creatures like eels
Gnashers	Teeth
Great Gurty	The biggest of all the gundiskumps
Grottish	Scary
Grubberlumpin'	Telling big whoppsy lies
Grumplet	A little beauty
Honourous	Honourable
Peepers	Eyes

Prawks	Like prawns but with bigger teeth
Prompty	On time
Rumpscallion	A nasty, rotsome bad guy
Sogsome	Damp and squishy
Spine-jangler	Something very spooky
Squiggers	Enormous sea slugs

Swashbunglers   Troll pirates, crooks and thieves

Swiggle   Gulp

Trollevator   A troll elevator

the Undersea   A big, wetty underground ocean

Yelpish   Frightened

Yonkers   Ages

Here's a few belly-bungling jokies to put you in a chirpish-type mood . . .

Q. Why couldn't Bilge, Spit and Blister play cards?

A. Because they were sitting on the deck.

Q. Which part of a gundiskump weighs the most?

A. Its scales.

Q. What lies at the bottom of the Undersea and shakes?

A. A nervous wreck.

Q. What is a gundiskump's favourite meal?

A. Fish and ships.

Q. How do you talk to a gundiskump at the bottom of the Undersea?

A. Drop him a line.

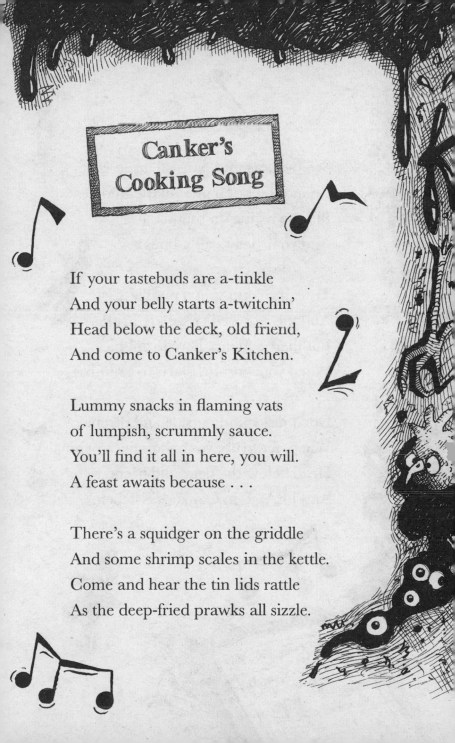

Canker's Cooking Song

If your tastebuds are a-tinkle
And your belly starts a-twitchin'
Head below the deck, old friend,
And come to Canker's Kitchen.

Lummy snacks in flaming vats
of lumpish, scrummly sauce.
You'll find it all in here, you will.
A feast awaits because . . .

There's a squidger on the griddle
And some shrimp scales in the kettle.
Come and hear the tin lids rattle
As the deep-fried prawks all sizzle.

See the pots and pans all jostle
Round the hot flames in the middle.
But the recipe's a muddle
And your belly's all a-bungle

True, the soup is in a puddle
And the seaweed crisps are brittle,
But there's plenty here to gobble
When your tummy starts to grumble.

Don't just stand outside and dribble
When, for grub, your chomper's itchin'.
Head below the deck, old friend,
And FEAST in Canker's Kitchen.

Honkhumptious news indeed! Not so long ago, all those brainy-bonks at Puffin Books held a whoppsy great competition to see who could come up with the lummiest, most tummy-tinkling troll menu. Lots of younglings from all over the place entered but there could be only one whoop-de-doop-de-winner!!

Congra-troll-ations to Hugo Mathew from Bedford Prep School for your squibbly trollicious menu . . .

~STARTER~
Pan fried barnacles drizzled
with puree of fish heads
accompanied by Rat fur
custard.
~MAIN · COURSE~
Lobster shells wrapped
in seaweed served with
a salad of seagull droppings.
~DESSERT~
Jellyfish eyes peppered
with newly hatched
wriggly maggots.

**My mouth is slobber-gobbin'
at the thought of it . . .**

DON'T MISS NEVILLE'S
FIRST ADVENTURE
UNDERNEATH . . .

AND ENJOY THE TROLLS' HILARIOUS VISIT TO THE OVERLINGS!

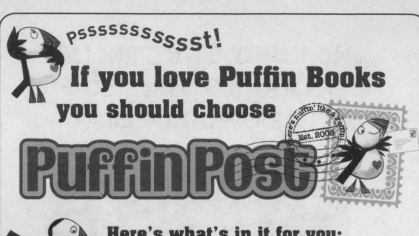

PSssssssssssst!

If you love Puffin Books you should choose

Est. 2008

Here's what's in it for you:

⭐ 6 magazines

⭐ 6 free books a year (of your choice)

⭐ The chance to see YOUR writing in print

PLUS

⭐ Exclusive author features

⭐ Articles

⭐ Quizzes

⭐ Competitions and games

And that's not all.
You get PRESENTS too.

Simply subscribe here to become a member
puffinpost.co.uk
and wait for your copy to decorate your doorstep.

(WARNING – reading *Puffin Post* may make you late for school.)